200 Ideas

for BDSM Sessi

Mistress – Slave

By Lady Sas

Frankfurt/Main, Germany, November 2017

Suitable only for adults who are open to topics such
as BDSM, fetish and sexuality. All actions are in mutual
agreement between adults.

Contents

Introduction

"Saskia, don't you have any idea what I could try out with my sub?", I am often asked. In this book I would like to give 200 answers.

My name is Lady Sas. For years now I have lived in Frankfurt/Main in Germany as a Femdom and I am intensively involved with BDSM. I not only write books about my personal experiences as a private dominant lady but I also keep a Femdom blog. In numerous interviews the Who's Who of the professional Dominas is presented and the Dominas answer my curious questions. I think it is my curiosity that drives me and helps me to keep coming up with new ideas and to follow new impulses.

So this book is about ideas on how to keep your BDSM relationship exciting and vibrant. Ideas keep each relationship fresh, interesting and varied. This is important, because otherwise even the most exciting love can turn into a paralyzing routine. The best way to build a stable relationship is to have fun, surprises and new ideas that you try out together. It is the little adventures, secrets and escapes from everyday life that unite and bring you closer together.

To help you I have put together 200 ideas for you to play exciting BDSM games. The selection is large, just try what appeals to you. From soft to hard, there is something for everyone.

What's exciting for the newcomer may be familiar to the experienced player. Nevertheless, I'm sure that there are also games in the selection that will put a smile on the lips of SM connoisseurs. It's all in the mix.

For better orientation I have divided the 200 ideas into categories.

SessionPlay: Ideas for a classic session between Mistress and slave.

Role-playing: Ideas for a different role and setting.

MindGames: Psycho games for the brain cinema.

Humiliation: Ideas on how to make the slave's cheeks blush with shame.

Chastity Control: Ideas for a slave wearing a chastity belt.

PartyPlay: Ideas for Femdom parties or games with several Femdoms.

You will find that some ideas can be grouped into several categories and sometimes they overlap. That's all right with me. The categories are only there to give structure and order to the book. This will make it easier for you to find your way around and, if necessary, to look up ideas.

Now have fun with 200 ideas for your next session. Be inspired and try something new!

Best wishes,

Lady Sas

PS: I translated this book from German to English. Please forgive me, if there should be mistakes, I am not a native speaker, but I did my very best.

I'd like to thank my test-readers for their help. I appreciate it! Thank you, Lady Liza, Victor, Simon, Patrick and Eric.

Indication of possible dangers

I would like to say a few more words about safety, which is particularly close to my heart. BDSM is a game - but in some areas it's not harmless. For example, in the case of breath play and control. A Mistress is responsible for the safety of her slave and has to make sure that he is well in every second. No one can relieve her of this responsibility.

Slaves are advised to hand themselves over only to Femdoms they trust and know that they are in responsible hands. Heart problems or health restrictions must be discussed openly before the session.

I would like to point out that this book does not encourage putting these ideas into practice. All information is purely informative. If you play BDSM games you play at your own risk.

I would ask all readers to only dare to approach games which they are sure to master and which do not overstretch any of the parties involved. It is not a sign of weakness to skip ideas but on the contrary a sign of maturity and sense of responsibility. Not all you can do is something you have to do. That is why the most important word in the BDSM play is "no". So: In case of doubt, just say "no" and be on the safe side. Thanks for reading this text. All right, let's get started.

Category SessionPlay

This category is about ideas for the session between the lady and her slave.

1. Impossible shoe kiss.

Impossible tasks are useful, for example, if the lady does not want to punish the slave without any reason, that is, if she is looking for a pretext.

The lady sits on the back of the slave who kneels on all fours. She crosses her legs and commands him to kiss her shoe. That's impossible because the shoe is too far from his mouth. The slave can also not move towards the mistress, because she sits on him. In short: This is an unsolvable task, which the slave cannot solve under any circumstances.

Now the mistress can savour the whole thing by repeating the order, threatening punishment and telling the slave what a useless worm he is. He can't even kiss her shoes – she's seldom seen anything so incompetent.

2. Impossible shoe kiss, bondage variation.

A variation of the impossible shoe kissing is to tie the slave and then demand a greeting from the other end of the room. A „greeting" in the BDSM-context is another description for the slave to kiss the lady's feet or shoes. The lady can for example tie the slave's hands and feet together. Simply connect the cuffs and ankle cuffs with a snap hook - that's it. Now the slave has to crawl laboriously to the mistress. He has to creep, roll or otherwise manage to reach her in order to comply with the order. Surprise: shortly before the slave has finally reached her, the mistress walks away.

3. Impossible blow job.

The slave gets the order to blow the strap-on of the mistress and to bring it to squirt. Since the strap-on is only a lifeless item it can never squirt.

The mistress now gives instructions on how to blow the strap-on. Obviously, however, the slave does not manage to suck the penis properly, because there will be no cum. The lady humiliates the slave and points out how incompetent and useless he is.

4. The perfect shade of red.

The lady instructs the slave to print different shades of red with a graphic program. Now the lady secures the slave and lets him choose a shade of red which pleases him.

The goal: The lady spanks the slave's ass until she has hit exactly this color red. An amusing idea that provides a lot of fun - even in a Femdom round. In practice, however, the red tone will barely be accurate so don't be disappointed. But it is precisely this that provides many reasons to punish the slave for this.

5. The wall parking lot.

It happens that you have to leave the slave alone for a while during the session. Maybe to get something. Or to take a little break.

In this case the lady has to "park" the slave somewhere - that's what I like to call it. Since not everyone has a cage, here is a simple alternative, which is also much more interesting: The slave has to stand directly in front of a wall and press an object with mouth and nose against the wall so that it does not fall down. For example, a paddle is ideal. The slave has to put his hands behind his back.

To make it even more difficult for the slave the mistress can also put a cane between his buttocks. If the object falls down the slave will be punished. A good way to fix the slave quickly and easily and keep him occupied.

Shoe fetishists can also have a high heel pressed against the wall. They then have the object of their desire right under their noses.

6. Leash on the testicles.

The lady puts a leash on the testicles of the slave. Now the other end of the line is attached to an object that cannot be moved even if you pull at it with all your strength. An iron ring or a solid railing would be perfect. A door handle can also work. However, I strongly recommend that you check beforehand whether the item really is strong enough.

The slave kneels on all fours to the ground. The leash from his testicles to the solid object should be stretched.

The lady stands before the slave and orders him to kiss and lick her high heels.

Now she slowly starts moving backwards. The slave must therefore stretch himself further and further to get to the shoes. Especially with high-heel fetishists this is a lot of fun because they really love shoes and will endure having their testicles stretched considerably. The lady goes back ever further until the slave is only able to reach the shoe tips with the tip of his tongue. In this position you can humiliate him wonderfully and show him how horny he is for the high heels of the mistress. In my experience a lot of slaves are fascinated by high heels and for most of them it is a strong fetish for which they will endure a lot.

7. High heel on the butt.

Take a seat on an armchair or sofa and let your slave lick your high heels until they shine. You place another shoe on his butt or his back which must not fall down while he is licking your shoes.

You can increase the difficulty level by, for example, working him over with the crop or asking him to blow your heel, which requires a different posture from him.

It would also be conceivable to let the slave crawl with the high heel on his back for a short while.

If all this doesn't help, you can also secretly just throw the shoe down yourself if he has bent his head deeply downwards. Instead of a shoe, you can also choose other item such as an ashtray made of metal. Only a fragile Ming vase shouldn't be considered.

8. Foot Challenge.

Sit on an armchair with your feet naked. Your slave kneels before you. Now instruct him to kiss your feet. Next, you put a foot in his mouth. Fuck his mouth pussy with your foot and tell him: "So, slave. Now your mistress will fuck your mouth pussy beautifully!"

After this foreplay comes the real challenge: How many toes of your two feet can the slave fit in his mouth? Put your feet close to each other on the floor and watch him. His job is to put as many toes in his mouth as he can.

If he really manages to get all your toes in, you mock him as a "big mouth" who never gets enough. If he doesn't make it, you call him incompetent and utterly useless. A loser all along the line.

9. Keep the line taut.

The slave is allowed to stand up for this game and is taken on a leash. His task is to ensure that the leash between him and the mistress is always tightly stretched.

The mistress walks around slowly in the room - and then suddenly makes steps towards the slave, who has to retreat accordingly fast, so that the leash remains stretched further. If the slave does not manage to react immediately, he will be punished. The whole thing is a kind of reaction test and tests how attentive and eager the slave is.

10. Heel fuck.

A very special pleasure is the ass fuck with the heel of a high-heeled shoe. But beware! This can easily lead to injuries because the anal area is very sensitive.

To make sure the game does not end with an anal fissure there are a few things to consider: The heel should not have sharp edges, it should absolutely (!) be wrapped with a condom and the anus of the slave should have been pre-stretched with a plug and made easily accessible with lubricant.

The slave kneels down and presents his buttocks to the mistress whereby he has to pull them apart. The mistress sits behind him on an armchair or chair. The best way is to let the slave put his forehead on the ground and warn him to stretch his butt out properly. This attitude is humiliating for the slave and invites you to take it up with verbal eroticism and make fun of it. The mistress can spit on the ass to make it even more slippery.

Then I recommend to inspect the slave's anus with a finger and to check if he is ready. The lady admonishes the slaves to immediately report if he should feel pain. Next, the mistress uses her high heel carefully and inserts the heel slowly and extremely gently. The mistress should make sure that she cannot slip off and sits safely and firmly on the chair. If you encounter resistance while inserting the heel or if the slave is in pain, please stop immediately.

In any case, it is important to describe exactly what you do to the slave. The coolest thing about all this is the idea to fuck the slave with the heel. The more violent the verbal eroticism turns out, the more intense the experience of the slave is. The game is above all a mental thing.

It would be wrong to fuck the slave a little bit and not say anything about it. That would be almost boring for the slave. The action lives from the fact that it sounds horny when you announce to fuck the slave with the heel. Warning: Please use this practice only if you are absolutely sure that you are not hurting the slave.

As preparation it is advisable that the slave cleans himself thoroughly with an enema.

11. Cum different.

The slave may jerk off and come - but he has to cum into his mouth. One way to do that is to place the slave against a wall. He has to lean against it with his back with his legs protruding upwards in the air. Now he has to slide his back and his butt up so that his penis points down to his mouth. He can jerk off and cum on command. He must hit his wide open mouth. If he doesn't hit the target, it's at least as entertaining and shameful.

12. Bell fun.

The mistress puts a little bell on the slave. For example, on the chastity belt, on a nipple or she ties it around the testicles with a string. It is important that the bell can hang and ring completely freely. The slave's task is to prevent exactly that. There must not be the slightest sound.

The slave must crawl through the room to get something for the mistress. The bell must not be audible. If the slave can't do that he will be punished.

Of course you can easily make sure that the bell will ring if the slave should become too skillful. Just step on his hand by chance - and the penalty points are his. Oops.

13. Figging pleasure.

The mistress puts a peeled piece of ginger into the anus (shaped like a plug). The ginger releases essential oils which cause a warm burning. His sex organs are supplied with more blood and his sexual desire is increased. The orgasm is also perceived more strongly and intensively in this state. The ginger's desire-increasing effect builds up quite quickly, within one to five minutes.

After the ginger has been removed from the anus, the effect disappears in about half an hour. This game is called figging and is ideal to be combined with a good spanking because with the ginger-butt-plug it is more difficult for the slave to tighten his buttocks, which in turn makes it harder to bear the blows.

14. Clamp challage.

The slave gets the task to attach 30 clothespins to his genitalia. If he manages to do it, the next session will be 40, and so on - until he can't manage any more and will be punished accordingly.

Variation and addition: In the second step, the mistress beats the evil, evil pins with a crop from the body. That can hurt and you have to aim well and precisely.

15. Special toilet brush.

There is a gag that has a very special attachment: the one of a toilet brush. It is great fun to equip the slave with it and let him clean the toilet in this way. For the sub, it is humiliating to have to dip his head deep into the toilet bowl to clean it.

You can watch closely and close the toilet lid without warning and flush water. You can push the slave into the toilet. Be prepared that he will try to pull his head out of its unsightly position.

After this game you can humiliate him by touching him unpleasantly and letting him know that he is spreading unpleasant smells. How embarrassing... Only for experienced slaves.

16. The ashtray.

The slave kneels attentively in front of the lady who smokes a cigarette. Whenever the mistress has to discard any ashes the slave rushes up, throws his head right back and opens his mouth wide, whereby he submits his tongue. The slave has to swallow everything and clean his tongue every time, so that he is ready for action again. Even cigarette butts can be disposed of in this very special ashtray if you have no health concerns.

17. Fire under your butt.

To make a fire under the back of someone is meant in a figurative sense and means to put pressure on someone. However, this idea actually means it literally.

A garden chair, which is made up of individual wooden strips with some distance between them is particularly well suited for this purpose. The slave sits on the chair. Directly under it candles are lit, as thick and high as possible. In this way the slave has actually fire under his ass.

The Femdom should try it out for herself first to get a feeling for it. It's an exciting and entertaining game but once you've tried it yourself, you'll find that you can't take the heat from a certain point on. Therefore the mistress should show mercy immediately, if the sub is no longer able to endure it. It can be dangerous if the slave has to endure the pain too long, so please: be careful.

18. Kiss the butt.

The slave learns how to best worship the mistress. He kneels naked behind her. His hands have to stay behind his back all the time. If the mistress is not sure whether he adheres to this rule she can fix his hands behind his back, for example by connecting his cuffs with a snap hook. She takes the slave on a leash and pulls him to her bottom. Now she instructs the slave how and where to kiss and lick her butt.

19. Take a seat.

The slave lies down on his back, the mistress takes a seat on his face. She chooses at will how much air the slave gets. This game is especially interesting if the slave was imprisoned for a while in his chastity belt and is accordingly horny for the mistress.

While the mistress makes herself comfortable, she can browse for example in a magazine. Of course, it is important to pay close attention to the signals of the slave. Try to pay careful attention to the slave and still give the impression that you hardly notice him.

Whether the mistress sits down with a leather skirt, a pair of trousers, panties or completely naked on the face, is left to her own discretion. A leather skirt is well suited, if the slave should not get air (see also the game "breath reduction").

20. Sandpaper fun.

The slave is rewarded because he may jerk off in front of the mistress but at the same time he must also suffer because he has to wrap a roll of sandpaper around his penis. It hurts and the skin turns red.

In general and with a bit of tact the idea with the paper is not dangerous and stimulating. Especially for the mistress of course.

21. Slave feeding.

The slave kneels in front of the lady, who sits comfortably on an armchair. She crushes the slave's food with her high heels and lets him lick the leftover food off the sole of her shoe. Bananas are well suited for example. You can also impale food with your heels and let the slave eat from the heels.

I recommend to keep a dog bowl of water ready, so that the slave can clean his tongue when it comes to licking the high heels of the mistress in the end, so that he can lick it again cleanly.

As an increase, you can refine the food in the bowl with spit or golden shower.

This game is especially exciting for shoe fetishists.

22. Turned off motionless.

If the lady does not need the slave, he can be put motionelessly in the following way for shoe fetishists: The slave kneels on all fours. A pair of high heels is put on his back. He can't let the high heels fall down. It is important to know that it is really strenuous in the long run not to be allowed to move. An even higher degree of difficulty can be achieved with clamps, weights, nettles or an anal plug.

23. Heel blisters.

The mistress sits on an armchair, chair or throne with legs crossed on top of each other. The slave now has to blow the heel of the shoe, which is in the air, like a cock. He has to take it deep into his mouth and spoil it with his tongue. Just like blowing a real cock. The whole scene is garnished with verbal eroticism of the mistress, who makes fun of him and tells the slave how she wants to have her heel sucked.

You can humiliate the slave here by praising him for how well he does it. If you can do this so well, you have practice and secretly sucked some real cocks...

24. Bastinado.

Often it is not possible leave marks on the slave. If the mistress does not want to give up punches bastinado is recommended. This is the term used to describe a stroke on the soles of the feet. This practice is very painful, especially when you take the cane. It's enough to have a crop to cause pain.

I recommend to touch slowly and carefully, as this practice is surprisingly painful for the slave. The big advantage is that there are no visible traces of this stroke practice.

25. Slapping.

Slapping the face is the quickest way to make clear to the slave who he is and what the role distribution between the mistress and him looks like. Once you have overcome yourself, most women enjoy it very much. You can deceive, stop the shot at the last moment or strike it unexpectedly. If you like to surprise him you can also blindfold the slave - so he never knows when he has to count on a slap.

It is important to hit the target and not hit the ear as this can damage the eardrum. Many beginners also hit the neck. It's not as bad as hitting the ear but it's still best to hit the cheek.

So: Gently push it until you hit it safely. Only then should you increase the strength of the punch. Again, it is good to be aware of the fact that you can hurt the slave if you hit him in the ear. One should respect this practice.

26. Ice cube pee.

Preparation: The mistress pours her golden shower (this is the SM-term for urine) into an ice cube tray and puts this overnight in the freezer.

Execution: The slave lies down on his back and is fixed in bondage. (I can't go into the bondage technique here, that would go beyond the scope of this idea book.)

Now the lady puts a funnel into the slave's mouth and fills the funnel with the golden shower ice cubes. Slowly the ice thaws and the slave has to swallow the ice cold golden shower of the mistress.

This idea is interesting if the lady does not want to supervise the slave all the time. The slave is busy - the lady has her rest.

For safety reasons the slave must be able to open the bondage himself if the mistress is not present. If the slave is reliable and you can assume that he is obedient, you can do without the bondage. The slave should also be able to spit out the funnel in an emergency.

27. Thrill.

The slave is fixed stretched out, for example tied to the end of a bed. Make sure the cuffs are taut. Then the slave is mercilessly tickled.

A nice game, especially in the run-up to a session, is to loosen the slave and to release tensions. Many slaves claim not to be ticklish. Don't let that stop you from trying. Sometimes that's just a protective statement to avoid the thrill.

28. Dice game.

The mistress lets the slave throw the dice himself to determine how many strokes he gets. She gives him one, two, three or four dice and the slave may throw his punishment himself.

To make the whole thing even more interesting, the mistress can place six different BDSM instruments in a row next to each other and number them. The slave first of all throws a dice to get the instrument with which he is given his punishment - and in the second step the number of strokes.

In this way the slave of the mistress can make no accusation if he is severely punished and leaves the session with marks. After all, he rolled the dice himself and is responsible for everything, so to speak. The mistress can wash her hands in innocence. She only implemented what the slave diced.

29. SM push-ups.

There's nothing like a muscular, trained slave! This idea promotes the fitness of the sub. He does push-ups under difficult conditions. For example, the mistress can sit on his back while he struggles. It is more motivating if the lady stands directly in front of the slave and he may kiss alternately the left and the right shoe with each lowering of his body.

30. High-heel mask.

This idea is particularly suitable for high-heel lovers. The lady puts a worn high heel over the nose of the slave and fixes his very special mask with a bondage rope or a leather band, so the slave can constantly inhale the scent of the lady's feet. For example, he can clean the floor or massage the feet of the mistress.

31. Ice cubes and wax.

The alternating use of ice cubes and candle wax is stimulating for the sub. Inexperienced femdoms should be careful with the wax, as this can hurt. It is best to test the wax on your own skin first and let the wax fall from a suitable height. The longer the hot wax is in the air, the better it cools down. Watch out for fire too. It is not desired that the carpet catches fire through a clumsy movement and the fire brigade has to be involved in the game.

If the slave is first treated with wax, his eyes blindfolded and suddenly a glass of cold water is poured over him, this is a shock to him. At first he will think that he has been covered with hot wax. The mistress has to weigh up whether she wants to put the slave through this shock. If he has a weak heart? Then maybe not such a good idea.

32. Slave shave.

The lady shaves the gentitals of the slave. The lady must concentrate, because a razor is extremely sharp and the slave (and his sensitive parts) is 100% in the hands of the mistress. For the slave this is a great thrill. He is completely under the control of the mistress and is at her mercy. This feeling is intensified when the slave is tied up motionlessly.

33. Foil bond.

The slave is fixed with a transparent foil, while lying on his back. The film is wrapped around his body over a large area. Then the slave's head is wrapped with the foil. He has to hold his breath for a moment and wait until the mistress has made a hole in the foil where his mouth is.

The lady sits down on an armchair and places a shoe on the mouth of the slave or on the opening in the foil. Only when she removes her shoe can the slave breathe again.

Safety information: This game is dangerous and should only be played with responsible and experienced participants. The slave should be able to free himself if necessary.

34. Golden shower.

The slave must kneel in the shower with his eyes blindfolded. The mistress stands over him and urinates on him. This practice is considered humiliating. But there are also slaves who regard golden shower as a reward and are also eager to consume this.

The challenge for the mistress is often to have to pee on command. This requires some practice, but this is quite normal, and over time it becomes easier. Beginners are especially excited in this situation, so much so that suddenly nothing works at all, although they have a full bladder. The best remedy is to take it calmly, to breathe deeply and not to put yourself under pressure. It's better to have the attitude: If it works, it's good, if it doesn't work, then it's fine too. In this way, the pressure slightly is reduced.

If the mistress wants the slave to receive the golden shower, she can put a funnel in his mouth so that not a single drop of the precious sparkling wine is lost.

The taste of urine depends on the diet. Coffee, for example, produces an unpleasant taste. If you would like to do your slave a favour as to the taste, then it is advisable one or two days before to drink a lot of natural water and if possible eat fish and vegetables.

35. Fisting.

Here is a game for advanced players. Fisting means that the mistress penetrates the slave's anus with her fist.

First, a finger is inserted into the anus, best done very slowly and carefully with a lot of lubricating gel and fisting grooves (special gloves). The mistress has to take a lot of time and stretch the slave bit by bit. It makes sense to stretch the slave before fisting by having him wear a butt plug, and then everything goes much faster. An enema for preparation is also recommended.

Gradually the anus is stretched with more and more fingers, until finally the mistress's entire fist disappears in to the slave's anus. In order to reduce the risk of injury, the mistress must proceed slowly, sensitively and carefully and take her time.

Slaves inexperienced with anal play cannot usually be fisted, they are simply too tight. In such a case the slave must first be prepared step by step for the fist. For example: with regular insertion of fingers, figging, strap on and prostate massage. It would be completely wrong to want to impose a whole fist on an anal newcomer. The anal region is very sensitive and injuries can occur if you do not act sensitively and cautiously or if you want to do too much at the same time.

36. Strapon.

The mistress wears a strap-on. The slave kneels submissively in front of her and has to blow her penis. Then the sub is taken in his anus with the strap-on. It is recommended to stretch the slave with a butt plug and prepare him for the strap-on. The strap-on itself is used with a condom and has been made slippery with plenty of lubricant.

The danger of injury is considerable, if the lady proceeds too fast. She has to take her time and sensitively stretch the slave until he is ready for the strap-on. Especially slaves who do not have any experience with anal play have to be handled carefully and step by step. You can't force it.

37. Dildo Challenge.

The lady introduces a dildo to the slave. Make sure that the condom in which the dildo is placed is well lubricated. Don't let him slip out! The more liquid gel the mistress has used, the more difficult this task is.

Now the slave gets a second task. Best of all one where he has to move. So for example: clean the floor in the kitchen, slave! Or: Crawl around me and kiss my high heels from all sides, slave!

If the dildo slips out, the slave will be punished by blows. If you want to increase the difficulty further, you can also put a dildo in the slave's mouth, which also has to stay in place.

38. Outdoor.

It's beautiful outside. Why stay in the apartment or party room when you can play outside? In order to maintain anonymity, it is advisable to visit remote woodland or an abandoned factory building early in the morning. The slave can also wear a mask in case someone should encounter you. You can protect yourself with a hat and sunglasses.

If you want to take a walk with your slave, you should buy knee pads. Well padded, otherwise you won't enjoy this walk. The slave will moan at some point and progress very slowly. Best of all, he is completely naked, wears only a chastity belt, his collar and the knee protectors. The mistress takes him on a leash and leads him behind her like a puppy on all fours.

What should you do if you actually meet someone? In this case, I recommend that you just go on and greet politely, as if you really don't have a slave on a leash, but a little doggy. If you have your car within easy reach and can flee quickly before being discovered, you can also choose this route.

There are many outdoor games where you can enjoy yourself. For example, you can send the slave into a lake. It's a matter of attitude. It is clear that outdoor games are more enjoyable in summer than in winter, but I have been out in the snow with my slave. And yes, he was naked. However, this is only recommended if the slave is able to work under pressure. Under no circumstances should the sub be exposed to the cold temperatures for too long, otherwise there is a risk of hypothermia. Here too, a sense of responsibility by the mistress is required.

39. Forbidden forced orgasm.

The slave is secured by the mistress and gets strict prohibition of ejaculation. Now his penis is stimulated by the mistress, for example with a Magic Wand massage device. This goes on until the slave has to cum. He's being coerced. Spraying without permission of the mistress? You can't do that! Thus he must be severely punished.

40. Tunnel games.

The picture of a tunnel should show that there is no way out once you get involved in the game. You can't break off and have to finish travel to the end of the tunnel.

One example of this is bringing the slave into contact with nettles. That hurts! And you can't undo it. As long as the slave has no allergic reaction to it, nothing dramatic should happen with nettles.

Another example of a tunnel game is to give the mistress the key to a chastity device and agree that the slave will receive it by via mail following week.

41. Pressure & Pleasure.

This task can be carried out by the slave at home without supervision. The goal is to make him think of the mistress even when she is not there.

The slave gets sexy photos of the mistress and may masturbate before these photos as often and as long as he wants. But: Under no circumstances, however, must he climax. This constant horniness, which results in jerking off even more, will soon be seemingly unbearable for the slave. There will be enormous pressure on him, so that he really has to pull himself together, not to cum by mistake.

42. WC idea.

This game is extremely amusing and entertaining for the mistress. The slave is instructed by her to drink a lot of water in the best style and as it should be from his dog bowl. Drinking, drinking, drinking, drinking is the order of the day.

As soon as the bowl is empty, the mistress refills fresh water. When she's generous, she garnishes the water with her saliva. She can also serve a urine spritzer with the water. The important thing is that the slave really drinks a lot.

Fine, the slave has to kneel now in the slave position. Upper body upright, legs slightly spread, hands with the palms upwards on the thighs, eyes submissively lowered.

Soon he will have the need to go to the toilet. But that is exactly what the mistress forbids him to do. An extremely unpleasant feeling, as anyone can imagine.

This evil game can be enhanced by forcing the slave to drink more. It is especially critical if the slave wears a pair of trousers and wants to avoid peeing without permission.

If the slave has to urinate without permission and is no longer able to keep himself under control, this naturally requires severe punishment and verbal humiliation.

43. The Hotel Window.

A game with the shame of the slave: When mistress and slave stay overnight in a hotel, the naked slave is only displayed with a mask "dressed" in the window of the hotel. It is advisable to choose a hotel situated in the middle of the city and facing a building.

While the slave is standing in the window, the lady can inflame his imagination by telling him that opposite is a shared flat with young female students who are looking forward to making fun of him. The lady can now pretend to call the students and have an alleged conversation.

The additional idea of making such a phone call with a friend is extremely amusing. The slave must not know the girlfriend or her voice otherwise he will be aware that he is being set up.

In the telephone conversation you can have fun with the slave and your friend can pretend to see him from the window. The slave will be embarrassed, too and try to see if there is anyone vis-à-vis. This can be sensually escalated and much more effective, if the lady blindfolds the slave's eyes. Then his senses are completely focused on the phone call.

44. Under power.

The slave provides the mistress with a power supply, which is attached to the genitals of the sub and triggered by the mistress via remote control. Prepared in such a way the lady goes out with her slave. For example: to a fine restaurant, theatre or opera. It can be anything, but no BDSM entertainment, because this game is all about the charm of what is hidden and secret. The mistress can remind her sub at any time, according to her whim and desire, painfully of who is in charge.

I recommend that you test the device before going out and do not set the current surges too violently. The health of the slave must also be paid special attention to here. It is better to approach this carefully and test it calmly than to experience nasty surprises.

45. Breath reduction.

In order to make clear to the slave that he is completely in the hand of the mistress, the mistress determines even the air the sub breathes. For this purpose the slave is bound motionlessly. The mistress holds his hand over his mouth and nose and ensures that he has to hold his breath. She can also sit on his face (face sitting, queening) and take his breath away.

The lady has to pay attention to signals of the slave. Breath reduction should only be carried out with a responsible mistress who can be trusted. The lady should inquire first about heart diseases or health restrictions. Please take care.

46. Guess the instrument.

The lady blindfolds the slave's eyes. For example: with a scarf. Now the slave has to kneel down on the ground and submissively stick out his butt. Because of his blindfolded eyes, the slave can now concentrate even better on what he feels. His task is to guess with which instrument the mistress chastises him. If it is wrong, he collects further penalty points, which are dealt with strokes (cane, whip or hand).

47. Cock and Ball Torture (CBT)/Ballbusting.

This is the torture of the genitals. For this the lady can for example use her fingernails. The testicles of the slave are particularly sensitive. A courageous kick in the balls - and the sub knows who's in charge.

However, the soft tissues are sensitive and inexperienced femdoms should feel their way to this game. For example, it is a good idea to try kicking the testicles without shoes.

48. Tease & Denial.

In this game it is about teasing the slave first, so to make him horny first - and then to deny him the satisfaction at the last moment and force him to fail (denial). It's a constant up and down, a constant game, with desire and the hope of salvation. Experts can maintain this tension throughout the session. All the more intense is the orgasm of the slave at the end of the game, when all the accumulated energy is finally allowed to be released.

The lady can tease the slaves with almost everything: Feet, shoes, hands, mouth, and breasts - everything is allowed.

49. Suck the banana.

The slave has to blow a peeled banana. In doing so, he has to be careful not to touch the banana penis with his teeth or even to "injure" it, so far, so good. It becomes difficult, if the lady issues the slave slaps to the left and right of the face. If the slaps come fast and hard, the slave may lose his mastery and bite. The banana is examined by the mistress for traces of his teeth. If there are marks, an unusual punishment and intensive blast of training is inevitable.

50. Potency analysis.

The potency analysis works like this: The slave has 30 minutes time to shoot as often as he can. He kneels down in front of the mistress and jerks off while the mistress amuses herself about his lust. No matter how often the slave manages to reach the climax, his mistress remains dissatisfied with his performance. He's gonna have to lick his mess up at the end.

The mistress can carry out this exercise once or twice a month if she keeps the slave chaste. In chastity, it is important to train the sexual apparatus of the slave regularly, otherwise impotence threatens.

It is also nice to do this potency analysis at a party.

51. Trampling.

The slave lies down on the ground and the mistress climbs up on top of him, runs around on him and makes so descriptively clear who is mistress and who is slave. At this point it is important for the mistress, not to overdo it and to be careful.

52. Weights.

The mistress weighs down the testicles and/or the nipples with weights. It is also interesting to bind a bucket to the slave's testicles and to fill it with water. Thus it becomes more and more difficult for the slave to maintain sublime attitude and withstand the pressure.

53. Bizarre shopping.

The slave accompanies the mistress to a shopping outing, carries her shopping bags and pays her bills. He gets nothing but sweet humiliations in return.

54. The yes-man.

The slave may only reply to all questions only one answer: Yes, mistress.

A "No" no longer exists; it is deleted from the vocabulary and must not be used by the slave.

This results in an interesting situation for the mistress. She can ask, for example:

Do you want to be treated really hard today, slave?

Would you like to jump over your shadow today and taste the champagne of the mistress?

Are you a stupid fool who only thinks about wanking?

Are you even too stupid to lie?

No matter what the mistress asks - the slave must always answer with "Yes, mistress".

A taboo remains a taboo.

But I think it's allowed to play with it and pretend to want to break a taboo, but not to do it in the end. It is interesting how the slave reacts to the announcement.

This procedure is however only something for slaves, who already have confidence in the lady. Otherwise the slave may abort the session because he is afraid that the mistress could really break the taboo. In this case, you can't blame the slave. His behavior is understandable.

55. The long dildo staff.

The cleaning slave kneels on the floor and cleans. The mistress steps behind him with a long dildo staff and instructs him to stick out his butt. She spears him anally and can now point him via the staff to where he should clean. The slave is pushed back and forth by the mistress. The whole thing is similar to a mop - except that you don't put a cloth on the dirty floor, but a cleaning slave.

56. The sub-up training.

There's nothing like a well-trained slave with a six-pack. To remind him of this, the mistress conducts a sit-up training: I call it the sub-up training.

For this the slave lays down on his back, the mistress sits down in an armchair next to him. She crosses her legs. And in such a way that there is a high heel in front of the slave's head. The slave must do a sit-up, i.e. raise up to be able to kiss the mistress's heel. A good work out! strenuous for the sub, but entertaining and comfortable for the mistress.

57. Sort shoes blind.

A fine game to keep the slave occupied for a while. The lady takes some shoes and places them before the slave. Now she blindfolds the slave's eyes and mixes up the pairs of shoes. She mixes the shoes and asks the slave to bring the matched shoes together and put the shoes in order. While the slave is busy, the mistress can dedicate herself to other things. After a certain time the mistress comes back into the room and observes the result.

58. The Cockbox.

A cock-box is a small, low table with a hole through which the slave puts his penis. The slave lies underneath the cock-box and is tied up, if the mistress wants to make sure that he does not resist.

Now the mistress can tease his penis with her feet or with her shoes. The cock-box is ideal to ruin the orgasm for the slave. The lady irritates the slave until he can no longer control himself and asks for permission to ejaculate. The mistress allows it (or doesn't) and stimulates him for a moment - but then pulls her foot back as soon as the slave cums. The slave comes to the climax, but has no satisfying feeling.

Note: This practice can be extremely dangerous, especially when sharp heels are in play. They can easily injure the penis. The lady must proceed extremely carefully. Their weight can also crush the penis and injure it. I advise slaves to only play this game with experienced mistresses.

One way to avoid accidental slipping with high heels is to sit in front of the cock-box in an armchair.

59. Impossible answer.

We have already had fun about the concept of impossible tasks. Another nice possibility for an impossible task is to gag the slave and then ask him questions. They should be open questions, not questions to which he can answer with "yes" or "no", because he could also express this with a nod or shake his head.

For the fun to be perfect, he has to be so tightly gagged that you really can't understand his grunted sounds at all. It is helpful, for example, to stuff a pair of worn pantyhose into his mouth and then gag his mouth. Now the slave cannot answer the questions at all. In other words, he refuses to answer! A downright insolence to which there is only one reaction: severe punishment. That's a good thing: Since the slave is already gagged, you don't even have to hear his wailing during the punishment.

60. The raw egg.

The lady demands from the slave to take an intact, raw egg in the mouth. His task is to show the mistress the egg unharmed later on.

The mistress now tests his self-control by punishing the slave. This can be done in many different ways. For example: firstly to warm up with your hand, then with the paddle, the crop and as the finishing touch with the cane.

It becomes even more difficult for the slave, if the mistress slaps him.

Can he save the egg from any damage?

In this game you should be careful to feel your way up first. The slave should first of all honestly say if he can even hold the egg in his mouth. He shouldn't choke on it, it can be really dangerous.

61. The short session in the elevator.

The elevator is a place that is often fantasized about in the sexual context. What vanillas (people without SM desires) call the quickie in the elevator; this is for BDSMler the short session in the elevator.

To do this, mistress and slave must be alone in the elevator. At least I would strongly recommend that... As soon as the door is closed, it starts. The beautiful thing about this is that the most diverse scenarios are conceivable. For example, the mistress can demand that the slave falls to the ground and licks her dirty boots clean. Or the slave has to kneel down and get his penis out in no time at all, jerking off and Cuming.

A lot of things are conceivable. The main attraction is the danger of being caught. In order to avoid embarrassment in case of a problem, you should not choose the elevator in your own company.

62. The Domina Dinner.

The lady orders the slave into the kitchen, because she wants to cook for him. But Domina Dinner quickly turns out to be anything but delicious. The mistress puts a dog bowl on the floor and fills it with all kinds of delicacies: mustard, ketchup, pepper, salt, spit, strawberries, blueberries, yoghurt, and beetroot - maybe even golden shower, i. e. urine. There are no limits to your imagination. The lady binds the slave's hands behind his back and wishes him a good appetite. If the slave is not enthusiastic enough to feed himself, the mistress can push him energetically with her hand or the foot into the bowl.

In order to stimulate the slave's appetite, the mistress can order the slave to skip lunch on the day before the session. You should leave the slave completely in the dark about the details of the dinner. All he needs to know is that he can look forward to a delicious dinner, which the Mistress will prepare especially for him. Lucky slave!

63. The Post-Orgasm Fun.

We all know this from men: they have achieved their goal; they have come and now want only one thing: their peace and quiet.

This is where the mistress comes in. She does exactly the opposite: she stimulates and stimulates the penis. Especially then, when she has brought the slave by jerking or with a massager to a climax but then simply continues as if nothing had happened, it is almost unbearable for the slave. It hurts him and he's going to twist back and forth. Therefore, it is recommended to fix him accordingly.

Amusing and entertaining: the slave comes to a climax, but the mistress pretends not to have noticed it. She then encourages him to finally release his juice and even increases the stimulation. This is both mentally and physically painful for the slave and the mistress should be prepared for some protests. But no problem: There are gags.

64. Electric play.

No, the "E-pulse" has little in common with a conventional stun gun (as used by the police on television). He's far too weak for that. Nevertheless, the electro-rod is powerful enough to spread fear and terror into slaves. The lady has thus an instrument in the hand, with which she can control and intimidate the slave.

Where will the mistress use the device next? on the arm, the thigh, nipples or perhaps not directly on...?

It is entertaining to watch how the tied slave twists and turns to escape from the electro-stick.

In order to enable the mistress to better assess the effect, I strongly recommend that you test the effect yourself beforehand. Yeah, that's how much work has to be done. You deal with the e-pulse in a completely different way when you have experienced its effect yourself. Weak-hearted slaves should be better spared this kind of play.

65. Ballet Heels.

Ballet Heels are extremely high boots or shoes. The special thing about them is that the extremely high heel leads to a maximum stretching of the foot. That reminds me of ballet shoes, hence the name. Shoes of this kind are fetish shoes. It is extremely difficult to walk with ballet heels. Often they are worn only for the session. Ballet Heels are worn by men and women. With a slave, you can use them well to feminize him even more. Running training is an amusing pastime.

However, one should proceed slowly and give the slave time to adjust to the heels. I recommend practicing falling first in order to show the slave to what he should do if he loses his balance. So you shouldn't tie the slave's hands, he has to be able to support himself while falling.

66. Spike Shoes.

An idea for slaves who do not wish visible traces of the session left. The sub wears spike shoes. These are shoes with small Spikes, which drill into the soles of the feet with every step.

The difficulty level can be increased if the mistress attaches a spreader bar to the ankle cuffs of the sub and carries it behind him on the leash. But you shouldn't pull on the leash; otherwise the slave might lose his balance. The slave can only move slowly in this manner and circumstantially/cautiously. It's not bad will, it's the spreader bar and the spikes.

In the disarray, spike shoes are bothersome, annoying and a little painful, but not dangerous.

67. The blindfold.

Men are visual beings. They like to watch. And we women have a lot of things to watch. How cruel for the lady taking this pleasure from the slave and putting a blindfold on him, a black silk scarf for example.

To have to survive such a session is a real punishment for the slave. Most people don't like it they would love to see the mistress and can hardly resist protests.

This state can be used very well. For example, with surprising slaps. Or a sudden kick in the crown jewels. Especially slaves, who think that they can withstand anything and think they are really tough guys, can literally be caught unprepared with this trick.

68. The penis line.

It's not unusual to put a slave on a leash with his collar. Leashing him on his best piece, on the other hand, is. In this way, he becomes aware at every moment of who leads and controls him and his sexuality.

This can be put into practice, for example, with a chastity belt. The lead is attached to the belt's lock. Experienced ladies can tie penis and testicles with a nylon stocking, so giving him bondage to the extremities. However, this is only for experienced femdoms, because the blood must be able to circulate further and if you don't know your way around, you can damage the penis.

A connection of this kind has a high symbolic character and is also perfect for presenting slaves at parties. However, this guaranty is obviously only for hard-boiled subs.

69. The nylon seam path.

Seamed nylons not only look erotic, they are also suitable for a little concentration game. The lady instructs the slave to kiss her along the seam along the legs from bottom to top, only at the seam! If the slave touches another place with his lips, the mistress immediately slaps his face.

It is funny when the slave kissed exactly along the seam, but still gets a slap in the face. Stupid for him, because if he refuses to admit his guilt, he will only make things worse and the punishment will be even more severe. He has no choice but to confess everything and to hope for mercy.

70. The Smoking Queen.

In the dazzling world of BDSM there are slaves who like to see their mistress smoke, for example thick expensive cigars. I don't know where this fetish comes from, but it excites the subs to observe their mistresses like that.

They kneel in front of the mistress and hold an ashtray ready, or open at the wink submissively their mouth as far as possible so that the Smoking Queen can deposit the ash into their mouth. Whether a mistress or a slave finds this exciting or not, one cannot tell, one must try it out. It is particularly exciting for the slaves when the mistress bends down to them and slowly blows the smoke into their faces.

71. The vice.

This idea serves to fix the slave for a strict punishment. Starting position: The slave kneels before the lady. The lady requests him to lower the head, makes a step towards the slave and clamps his head between the thighs. Firmly, really hard! Now she instructs the slave to stretch out his butt and spanks him calmly.

This position has two major advantages. For one thing, the slave is fixed/ bound. On the other hand, he enjoys the intoxicating closeness of his mistress during the punishment and is therefore motivated to endure the blows.

After a certain number of hard blows the slave will start to become restless and fidgety. In this case, it is advisable to change to the weight position described below.

72. Weight position.

The lady instructs the slave to lie down on his belly. She sits on his back, face, facing the buttocks and hits his ass. This position is very well suited to keep the slave in position. The entire weight of the mistress pushes the slave down, which lies comfortably - whereby the blows are certainly anything but comfortable for him. The proximity of his mistress should motivate him to endure the punishment.

73. Shut Up!

Especially in a new mistress-slave relationship or with still inexperienced slaves, the subs tend to speak without being asked. The mistress must make it clear to them that they have to keep their mouth shut and may only say something if the mistress asks them something.

To make this clear, the lady announces to the slave that his big mouth is going to be stuffed. But not with a normal gag, that would be too easy. She instructs the slave to take a particularly large dildo deep into his mouth and keep it in his mouth. If the dildo should slip out, she threatens a severe punishment. Now the lady can make fun of the fact that the slave can no longer say anything.

"You're suddenly so quiet? What's the matter with you? I don't know you that well. You're usually such a chatterbox."

If the mistress has the desire to punish the slave, she can ask him a question and then get upset because the slave has not answered.

The slave is in a dilemma. If he answers, he has to push the gag out of his mouth. If he does not answer, he will also be punished.

The gag should be really thick, so that the slave can't talk through it.

74. The high heel selection.

The lady would like to find out which of her high heels she wants to wear today. She sits comfortably in an armchair, the slave kneels before her. A pre-selection of shoe pairs is also available. Now the slave presents a pair of shoes. The lady looks at the shoes and instructs the slave to worship the shoes with tongue and lips. Which pair is mistress inclined to? Which heels are best suited to torment the slave with them? For which pair will the mistress decide? She has all the time in the world to test it out.

75. Keep the High-Heel in your mouth.

A concentration game: The slave is fixed to a cross and gets now a high heel of the mistress put in his mouth so that he has to hold it with his mouth at the tip. The mistress warns him, under no circumstances to bite on the shoe or to damage them with the teeth.

While the slave holds the shoe with his mouth, the mistress is tampering with the slave. She pinches him in the nipples, plays with his penis, attaches clamps to his nipples, hangs weights on his testicles, tortures him with wax or maybe even kicks him in the balls.

The slave has to endure everything and keep the shoe in his mouth.

If the mistress has no more desire, she goes and drinks a coffee or tea, while the slave holds the shoe in his mouth trying not to use his teeth.

At the end she finds out that tooth impressions can be seen on the toe of the shoe, scolds the slave and demands new shoes. It is completely irrelevant whether or not dental impressions are actually visible.

76. The cage tease.

A fine game for shoe and foot fetishists: The lady locks the slave into a cage. She sits on an armchair in front of the cage and places her feet comfortably on a footrest directly in front of the cage.

The slave will now do everything possible to get to the shoes or feet of the mistress. It is extremely entertaining to see how he presses himself against the bars and how long he can make his tongue to reach the object of his desire.

The mistress plays with his fetish, occasionally gives him a touch of her feet and then pulls them away again.

77. The cold shower.

Some slaves are sniveling sissies. Even a cold shower can scare them back. You can play with it to harden them a little bit. The lady places the slave under the shower and instructs him to place the water on ice cold. Brrrrr... Cold!

This can be combined wonderfully with a stimulating, hot cock-teasing beforehand, which ends just before the orgasm. The slave can be grateful that his mistress is so caring to cool him down again.

78. Slave tongue vs. shoe brush.

The slave has to clean the right leather boot of the mistress with his tongue. The left leather boot, on the other hand, has to be cleaned with a brush. If the right boot shines more than the left boot, it is punished for being negligent with the brush. If it's the other way round, he gets a punishment for being careless with his tongue. Either way, the slave always loses.

79. Footing.

We already got to know the practice of fisting. The mistress takes the slave with the fist anally. Footing is an increase: The lady takes the slave with her foot. Beginners especially may be surprised by this statement, but this game actually has many fans. Especially slaves, who have been taken anally for years, appreciate the extreme increase.

It is important that this game is only played with really experienced slaves who are physically fit for it. In my experience, it takes many months to anally stretch and prepare a slave in such a way that he can be footed.

Since there is a considerable risk of injury in the anal area, there is a lot to consider. Foot nails must be shortened to minimize the risk of injury. The mistress should pull a condom over the foot. Lubricant is an absolute must for footing. Patience and empathy are also important.

The slave must be brought into a stable position. For example, he can kneel on all fours in front of the mistress, who sits comfortably in an armchair behind him. The mistress can think about putting a mirror in front of the slave so that the slave is able to observe more of his treatment.

I recommend the mistress always describes what she is doing for the slave. For the slave it is very erotic to hear what the lady is doing with him. Furthermore, even with mirrors he will never see perfectly what is happening.

80. Kissing and licking away.

The mistress distributes plates in the room or in the whole apartment. She has left a beautiful kissing mouth with lipstick on every single plate. The slave has now the task to find all plates and lick away the lipstick kiss.

The goal: The lady strikes the slave with the crop throughout, until he finds all the kisses and licks them away. So she's driving him to hurry with the task. The mistress can change the crop at will, if she so wishes. She can also give hints like "Here it's getting hot" if she wants to help the slave or lead him astray.

81. The Venus 2000.

The Venus 2000 is a sex toy that can quickly bring men to an orgasm. In the receiver, air is alternately supplied and sucked off. This results in an up and down movement, which has a stimulating effect. But the whole thing only becomes interesting after the first orgasm, when the machine continues to run mercilessly and demands the next orgasm. The bound slave is unrelentingly milked - to the last drop.

How much juice can the slave give? When does the lust begin to hurt? With Venus 2000 you can find out. It is not necessary to buy the machine immediately. You can also rent them or rent studios or SM-apartments where they are available.

82. Memorize your slave contract.

The slave gets the task to learn his slave contract a little. If there is no contract, the lady sets up 10 individual slave rules. The slave gets these 10 rules handed out and has the task to learn the rules until the next session.

It is amusing to set the slave in panic and tell him that he has 10 minutes to memorize the 10 rules. He will react stressfully and it's fun to observe the next 10 minutes.

After that the lady asks the slave. What's rule 5, what's rule 9? Are you sure this isn't rule 8?

The mistress insists that the slave must reproduce everything verbatim, not only in terms of content. That makes it even harder for him. Of course, poor performance must be punished. The cane will motivate the slaves and help them to remember.

Here is an example of 10 slave rules. The list is for inspiration only. The more individual the 10 rules the better.

The slave has to serve the mistress and obey her under all circumstances.

The slave has no right to an orgasm. Only the mistress decides when and if.

The slave only has to talk when asked to do so. If he is asked something, he has to answer honestly and openly.

The slave must always be naked and on his knees when the mistress is present.

The slave has to maintain his body and keep in shape with sport. In the intimate area he must always be perfectly shaved.

The slave has to bear any punishment by the mistress gratefully.

The slave is exclusively bound to the mistress. Contacts with other women are strictly forbidden.

The slave has to regularly place gifts at the mistress's feet without being asked, in order to show her his worship in this way.

The slave can be presented to the mistress girlfriends, if she wishes.

The mistress is always right.

83. Foot feeding.

We already know the classical slave feeding. The slave eats the trampled food from the soles and heels of the mistress.

If he was a good boy, the lady can also reward the slave by dipping her bare feet in yogurt and letting the slaves lick the delicacy from her feet, a dream for every foot fetishist. The yoghurt can be enriched with fruit or cereals. A nice slave breakfast!

84. Passion of a slave.

The lady takes the slave on a leash and instructs the sub to crawl behind her. She holds the leash in such a way that the leash between her legs leads to the back of the slave's collar. Now she tightens strictly on the leash and instructs the slave to worship her butt with submissive kisses. If the slave slackens, the mistress pulls energetically on the leash. The interesting thing about it is that the mistress can directly influence the kissing and the passion of the slave through the leash. Dissatisfied with the passion? Just pull tightly on the leash.

85. The Golden shower inhaler.

You can get pee inhalers online. They are available in a wide variety of designs, but the principle behind it is always the same: The slave wears a mask, which is connected to a container with the mistress's golden shower (urine) in a tube. Many slaves find it exciting to take up the scent of the golden champagne.

86. The painful jerking off.

The lady secures the slave in such a way that he has a hand free and can jerk off. His bottom should also be accessible. A trestle is well suited for this.

Now the lady allows the slave to jerk off and even come to the climax. The catch to the thing: While he jerks off, he is rigorously whipped or at least beaten by the mistress. So he has to endure the pain and at the same time try to reach the climax quickly. The result is the ultimate pain of pleasure.

87. Toothbrush torture.

The lady fixes the slave, so that he is defenseless to her wishes. Now she takes care of his cock with a toothbrush. First she rubs it gently and agonizingly slowly over the glans of the sub, then more and more intensively... Ouch!

88. Ouch! Rubbing alcohol.

The slave is secured and defenseless. Now the mistress applies some rubbing alcohol on the glans. She can also fill a few drops into a condom and roll it over the agitated penis. It is important not to use too much of it, otherwise there is a risk of damaging the mucous membranes. Severe burning will be the result of this treatment. Important to know: The effect of natural substances is not always the same. It can be perceived more intensively and sometimes less intensely. I recommend that you start with only a little rubbing alcohol.

Category Role-playing games

The fascinating thing about SM is that you will find an unlimited playing field for your imagination. A playing field on which almost anything is possible.

89. Role play: Slave market.

The role-playing slave market is about the scenario that the lady goes to the slave market to buy a new slave. This situation reminds us of the circumstances in ancient Rome, where it actually existed. The mistress examines the naked goods, which have to endure everything - or which must be fought back and forced to kneel with the whip. Best of all, the slave is well fixed and defenceless when the mistress inspects and grabs him. She can humiliate the slave by not expressing herself enthusiastically about his body, demanding more muscles and doubting the functionality of his penis or amusing herself about his size.

90. Role play: Mistress – dog.

The slave slips into the role of a dog. This can be a cute little lapdog - or a sharp watchdog. As a dog, the slave may not walk on two legs, but must crawl on all fours. I strongly recommend knee pads for this. The thicker the padding, the better. Otherwise the slave will have little joy in this role.

The dog is not allowed to talk and can only bark. He learns to walk on the leash to heel and to wag his tail when he sees the mistress. If he does everything well, he might get a treat. If he pretends to be stupid, there's the dog whip.

A bowl of water should also be available. If you are tough, you can spend a night outdoors in the kennel - but I would only do that in summer. We don't want to overtax the dog.

A fine game in the game is to let the dog retrieve things.

91. Role play: the whore.

The slave is dressed up as a TV and feminized. Now begins a detailed whore workout. Many men think about being a whore and earning money for the mistress. In 99.9% of the cases this is only a fantasy and not meant seriously.

The mistress trains the whore and teaches her to blow her strap-on and let herself get fucked properly. She shows the future whore how to present herself on the sidewalk and helps her to dress up in slutty clothes and make up herself sexy.

92. Role play: Mistress – tail girl.

This is about questioning the masculinity of the slave and humiliating him as a tail girl.

The lady puts out behaviours and characteristics of the slave as unmanly and almost typically female. His lips are very tender, his skin is very soft, his neck as graceful as a woman's. In the end, the mistress suspects, the slave is not a man at all, but a girl.

The tail girl gets a female name (from Marc becomes Marcella for example). She is ordered to go to the ladies' department, to dress like a sexy girl and to photograph herself in the mirror of the changing room. The tail girl has to hold a note on which it says: Lady Y's tail girl X.

93. Role play: officer – prisoner.

The mistress takes on the role of the strict officer, who does everything possible to elicit his secret from the prisoner or to persuade him to confess. The officer interrogates the prisoner and uses various punishment techniques to persuade him to surrender. This can be, for example, a classic punishment with a cane or whip. Or hot wax. Or nipple torment. Or Cock and Ball Torture (CBT). Or or or or or.

To reinforce the impression of the interrogation, the officer can light up the prisoner's face with a flashing desk lamp and put him under pressure. Food, cigarettes and sleep deprivation? The officer will know what to do. For example, if the prisoner is a coffee fan, she can enjoy a coffee in peace and quiet before his eyes, while he doesn't get anything to drink and has to watch. "You want a nice cup of coffee? No problem, tell me the secret and you'll get your coffee."

94. Role play: Instructor – recruit.

At military games, the mistress slips into the role of the nasty, strict instructor who drills the recruits in the barracks tone. Lonely forest sections are best suited for this purpose. Here, the trainer can chase the recruits through the bushes, send them into a pond or have them crawl through the mud.

"Go, go, go, go! Don't be lame, you wimp! This has to go faster! Go, go, go, go!"

95. Role play: teacher – pupil.

The pupil was cheeky and now has to be put over the strict teacher's knees. This role-playing game is especially popular with the older generation, who really felt the cane in school. A strict tone is part of it: "Snotty brat! You now write 100 times: I will never show the teacher my member again."

96. Role play: nurse – patient.

"Acute limb stiffening? Oh! We have to do something quickly. Get out of the way, Doctor X is going to check it out."

In this role play the lady slips into the role of a medical specialist, who examines the patient in detail. She should formally adhere to real medical terms and expressions in order to make the role-playing game look real. White clothing is obligatory.

"Probably a semen sample will also be necessary. Don't worry, it'll be all right. The doctor has a lot of experience with limb stiffening."

97. Role play: Governess – pupil.

Lovers of this role-playing game like to see the mistress in a strict, high-necked outfit. A long skirt, a buttoned up white blouse - this is the typical outfit of a strict educator who has to teach the cheeky boy manners.

"No, boy! No begging or pleading helps. Punishment must be! The yellow uncle will show you how to behave."

98. Role play: pleasure slave.

The slave has only one function: to give the mistress pleasure. She trains him to be her perfect pleasure slave and shows him how to satisfy her. The slave himself may only hope for satisfaction in the most exceptional cases. After all, it is not about his lust, but about the lust of the mistress.

99. Role play: Shoe and foot slave.

Most slaves have a fetish for the feet, stockings, high heels and boots of the mistress. It is a secret dream for them to be the private shoe and foot slave of the mistress.

In this role they are responsible for ensuring that all shoes of the mistress are as clean as lightning. They have to lick the shoes with their tongue and to care for the mistress's feet and massage them. Their whole being is all about one thing: the mistress's shoes and feet.

100. Role play: Object identification.

The slave is no longer a person, but an object. For example, a table. All you need is a wooden panel, which you put on the back of the slave crouching on the floor. You can now place things on this table top as you like. I would however suggest not to put up a valuable porcelain service, because it may well be that the slave is unable to do it any more or that the table top falls down due to an inconsiderate movement.

If you don't have a panel like that, you just take a tray. You can increase the difficulty even more by placing a ball or a high heel on the table, for example. If the ball rolls down or the high heel falls over, the slave has failed.

This task is very well suited to keep the slave occupied for a while. You can increase the difficulty even further by introducing an anal plug that must not slip out. If you put it on the plate that falls down, you can hit him on his outstretched butt until he can't control himself any more and the plate slides to the ground. Now you have a good reason to punish the slave even more. You can't let that kind of uncontrollability and poor performance go unpunished.

101. Kidnapping game.

The slave is kidnapped by the mistress. This can be done on an open road. For example, the sub should arrive at a petrol station at a given time. Suddenly he feels the barrel of a pistol in his back. It's just a toy pistol, but that doesn't matter, it's all about role-playing. The lady directs the slave to his car. He has to drive off, constantly threatened by the mistress with the gun.

One step further you go, if you put a sack over the slaves head, lead to the car and tie him up there. The bag should of course be designed in such a way that the slave gets good air under it. The idea of transporting the slave in the boot is only good if he gets air. Please pay attention to these points.

It is particularly exciting for the slave if he does not know where the kidnapper takes him, how long he is being abducted and what to expect. The lady should therefore absolutely try to leave the slave in the dark about these points. Insinuations that go in different directions bring the sub's imagination up to speed.

The mistress should consider why she kidnapped the man. What does she want from him? Is it about getting a secret out of him, for example? Even using constraint, pain and torture? The answer to this question determines the course of the game. An intense experience, that promises excitement and thrills.

102. Mrs. Doctor Strange.

The lady slips into the role of Dr. Strange, an ambitious scientist who researches the male instinctive behaviour. The slave takes on the role of a criminal who has actually been sentenced to 20 years in prison, but can hope for a pardon if he volunteers for the doctor's tests.

Now the volunteer has to surrender to the perverse games of the scientist and endure everything. After all, he wants to be pardoned and escape prison.

103. The punching bag.

The lady would like to keep herself fit with sport. This must be supported by her slave, of course. He is allowed to put himself at the disposal as a punching bag. The mistress gets herself boxing gloves and goes to train with her punching bag. Ouch!

So that the slave survives this, he should best tense his abdominal muscles as soon as the mistress trains on him. The athlete should be sporty and not box the punching bag in sensitive areas. If you use a little bit of sensitivity and don't exaggerate, the boxing session is a lot of fun. Masos in particular will get their money's worth. For pure devote slaves this kind of session is nothing.

104. AgePlay.

AgePlay stands for games with age. One is mature, experienced, powerful, while the other is young and inexperienced, uncertain and weak. The difference between young and old makes it easy to build a power gap. Examples of such installations are director - pupil, aunt - nephew or boss - trainee.

Important: It doesn't matter which age you actually have. The AgePlay also allows a 60-year-old child to take on the role of a pupil, who is cited to the headmistress' room and has to take a stand. In some cases, the desired castors are extremely distant from their actual age. Some men prefer to place themselves in the position of babies. Maybe to finally get the affection and attention they missed from their mother in the past.

105. PonyPlay.

In PonyPlay, the slave slips into the role of a horse. Particularly interesting in this area are the outfits, which contribute to the slave's perfect immersion in his role. There are horse masks or pseudomasks, harnesses, hoof boots, hoof gloves and tails which are fixed by anal plugging.

The pony is trained to show certain gaits on command and can also be harnessed in front of a buggy to draw the mistress. Buggy races between several teams are popular.

If you don't have such a car, you can have the horse trot on all fours. If you have a saddle for that, that would be even better.

In another variant the mistress climbs on the horse's shoulders. However, there is a particular risk of injury to the back of the sub-subject. Riding crop, whip and bridle are often used to promote dressage success.

It is obvious that a horse cannot speak and does not sleep in a bed, but in the stable. You can play through this role reversal consistently - up to the food: So a good little horse gets water, apples and sometimes a piece of sugar.

106. Breeder – Stallion.

The dominant breeder would like to take a sperm sample from her stallion to find out how well he is suited for breeding. So the stallion is fixed. Then the breeder starts to stimulate and milk his cock. Let's see how much sperm the stallion has to offer.

107. Thief – department store detective.

The slave slips into the role of a thief who has been caught in the act by the department store detective. Now she demands all sorts of perverted things from the man and blackmails him to hand him over to the police. Or worse still, informing his wife.

Let's go! On your knees! Kiss my shoes. You're mine now. And I can do anything with you that I want.

108. The four-legged friend.

With a sturdy belt you can easily transform the bipod into a house-trained quadruped. Just close the belt and put it on the ground. The slave kneels on the surface that surrounds the belt. Now the mistress pulls the belt up so that it is stretched between the ankles and the thighs of the slave. Knee pads are recommended, because knee crawling is strenuous and not healthy.

Such a beautiful little dog, the mistress should take him immediately by the leash. Let's go for a walk!

109. Strict aunt – youngster.

The aunt has to watch the boy. When she comes into his room to check up on him, she surprises him while secretly wanking in front of a porno movie on the computer. Aha! Caught in the act! The aunt will put you on your knees and drive out the nonsense.

110. The shrewd policewoman.

In this game, the lady takes on the role of a policewoman or commissioner, who investigates undercover and transfers the slave to act as a gangster. She confronts him with a toy weapon. The crook can now confess - or the policewoman has to help a little, put the gangster under pressure and maybe even grab a belt to hear what she wants to know. The state's monopoly on the use of force is being exhausted to the limit here. Escape is impossible. How far will the cop go?

111. The blackmailing boss.

British Conservative MEPs allegedly liked to visit Dominas in London at the time of Margaret Thatcher. In their imagination, they loved to submit to the strict Prime Minister. In short: A dominant boss exerts a strong attraction on submissive men. And all the more so when she is blackmailing and exploits her position to subjugate the man.

You want a raise? You want to take a vacation? Then do something about it! Here, my shoe is dirty. Clean it properly with your tongue. Get on the ground, now! Or should I give you Mrs. Braun's files for editing? You're gonna need a warning or what? There, there you go.

112. Broker – prospect.

Beautiful apartments are in great demand. And some men would do anything to get a good apartment. But: The prospective customers are queuing up, the real estate agent can choose who she wants to favour. She is now mercilessly playing off this power. She humiliates the interested party wherever she can.

Take off your clothes, you want to see who's here as a tenant. Of course, I have to see what kind of guy wants to move in here. Uh-huh, a submissive slave, soso. Well, get on your knees! Wanna see what the new tenant is for?

113. Burglar.

"Hands in the air! You are in my hands!" The harsh burglar leaves no doubt as to who is giving the orders now. She can tie up the man and dig around in his clothes. Who knows, maybe she'll find some embarrassing secret to blackmail the man? A secret porn collection? Photos of the colleague taken secretly? How embarrassing! Now the man is really under the control of the burglar and must do everything she asks.

It is best to play this role-playing game in the slave's apartment. It's really fun to search the place.

114. Colleagues.

The lady takes the role of a woman who blackmails her colleague. The colleague notices that her colleague stares at the high heels with a twist and invites him to kneel down in front of her and lick her shoes. In this pose she takes pictures of him. Now she has the colleague in her hand. She threatens to publish the photos on the notice board if the man doesn't do what she wants. He has to strip naked, masturbate in front of her and kiss her butt. But that was just the beginning....

115. Gynaecologist – tail girl.

The slave becomes the tail girl, who wears feminine lingerie and is examined by the gynaecologist with a speculum. Sterile disposable vaginal specula can be bought online. The doctor examines the cock girl's butt pussy, checks the tail for functionality and takes a sperm sample.

Health advice: The specula must be disposed of after use to avoid cross-contamination and infection transmission. Do not reuse.

116. Macho – Housewife.

In this role-playing game, the cliché roles of man and woman are exchanged. The lady slips into the role of a macho, the slave into the role of a submissive housewife - gladly also with female clothing, facial expressions and supporting gestures.

The mistress can invite a friend and let the housewife serve the coffee. Such a change of role is extremely entertaining.

Category MindGames

Sex starts in the head. BDSM too. Most slaves are less into pain and more into psychodrama and sweet humiliations. They love to be dominated and to be humiliated by their mistress. The feeling of being at the mercy of the mistress kicks him off. In this category we look at some MindGames.

117. Fake beatings.

Fake punches are punches that hit their target in the slave's head, but not in reality. The whole thing works like this: The lady connects the slave's eyes. He has to kneel down in front of a sofa and bend over at the front. Then the mistress takes a percussion instrument, which the slave fears. Maybe he is a beginner who has never felt the cane in all its hardness? Before the Sub is blindfolded, he may take a close look at the cane in this case. He may take it in his hand and feel how strong and flexible the cane is. The idea is to build a dramatic, threatening and very painful scenario, but at the decisive moment not to beat the slaves, but to hit a cushion on the sofa.

This procedure can be compared to a sham execution, which also causes extreme tension and anxiety. Sure, with the fake hammers, the sub doesn't have to be scared to death. But nevertheless this punishment is very intensive for the slave's imagination. He will be extremely grateful to the mistress for having spared him.

The mistress can leave the slave a few minutes in the ambiguity whether the punishment is still coming or whether she will only work the pillow next to him today.

He can never be sure what she's up to and what she's planning next.

In the end, if it turns out that the mistress is merciful and does not beat him, the mistress should in any case point out how generous she was and how grateful the slave must be to her.

118. Bell strike.

Only suitable for slaves who have no heart problems. The lady fixes the slave elaborately in the middle of the living room. It must be clear to the slave that it will take him a few minutes to be released. Now the lady can load the slave's nipples with weights, introduce a plug and add other refinements.

The mistress leaves the room for a moment and announces that she will be back in a moment. She takes off her high heels outside and sneaks out to the doorbell and presses it. The slave will get quite a fright!

It is also conceivable that the lady agrees on a fixed time with a girlfriend, at which the girlfriend rings at the door. The slave will be frightened. The mistress' visit is in front of the door, but it will take some time until the slave is freed.

The mistress can also invite the girlfriend in and show the helpless slave. Interesting, if the slave doesn't know about this action. But before you do this you should really think about whether you can take this step without asking the slave. Personally, I advise against outing the slave in front of people if this has not been discussed with him beforehand. However, if he has agreed in principle to be shown to good friends of the mistress, this scenario is conceivable.

119. Pharmacies idea.

This little game serves to humiliate the slave. The lady tells him to look around pharmacies for a pretty young saleswoman.

If he finds her, he has to tell the mistress about her. Now follows the second part of the game.

The lady commands the slave to ask the young pretty saleswoman for especially small condoms. It doesn't have to be so loud that everyone hears it, but the young lady has to hear it. If the lady would like to savour the humiliation on site and live, she can also be present in the pharmacy and pretend not to know the slave and look for something on the shelf.

This nasty little game will humiliate the slave to the extreme and hit him in his masculinity, because of course it is extremely embarrassing to confess to such an attractive lady that you have a particularly small penis in your pants. He'll sink to the ground with shame.

120. The pink ribbon.

The lady furnishes the slave with a pink ribbon tied in a bow, which she attaches to his CB or his tail. A small thing with great effect, because slaves hate this female symbol per se. All the more amusing for the mistress.

The humiliation becomes even more intense when the lady presents the slave girlfriends and she talks about the sweet pink ribbon. But be careful: For some men this is almost unbearable.

121. Floor instead of bed.

Especially in long-distance relationships it is important that the slave thinks about the mistress as often as possible. For example, an effective means is to instruct the slave that he/she can now only sleep on the floor. On the bed he has to deposit a photo of the mistress.

Or the slave may only shower cold. Or, he can only eat from the dog bowl. Of course without knives and forks, kneeling naked on the ground. In this way, the mistress is present - even if she is not in the room personally.

122. Abandoned in the forest.

The lady drives with the slave early in the morning into the forest. The day before, she found a reason to punish the slave severely. The mistress stops in a part of the forest, where if possible no strollers can be suspected. The slave takes off his clothes. He may only keep kneepads, his collar and - if available - his plug.

The lady sits down again at the wheel and commands the slave to kneel beside the car in front of the driver's door. She lets the window down and gives the slave a juicy lecture.

Then it starts slowly. The car rolls away very slowly. The slave will panic and wish to have not upset the mistress. If the slave is almost out of sight, the lady stops, waits briefly - and then lets the car roll back slowly. The slave may apologise and if the mistress is generous, she takes him along.

If strollers happen to show up, I recommend to drive away, if this is possible in time. If the strollers are already too close, one greets them politely as if nothing had happened.

123. A dilemma.

A dilemma arises when you give the slave two commands, which are mutually exclusive. This means that the slave cannot execute both commands and has to choose a task. However, he neglects the second task, which of course must be punished. The slave must experience unconsciously that he offends against the order of the mistress. He is helpless and can do nothing against his failure, even in the best of intentions.

So much for the theory. What does it look like in practice? The mistress can instruct the slave, for example, to keep his mouth shut, because he only talks nonsense anyway and she doesn't want to hear anything more from him today. Then she asks him a question. If possible, one that the slave cannot answer with yes or no, otherwise he could nod or shake his head. "What are you thinking about when you jerk off, slave?" Could be a question like that. The slave must answer contentwise. But that is exactly what the mistress had forbidden him shortly before. If he dares, the mistress rejects him rightly if he is deaf, as she had expressly forbidden him to say anything today. If the slave silences, however, he immediately gets a juicy slap in the face, because he does not answer to a direct question. The slave is in a dilemma and can only lose this game.

If he makes the mistake of arguing rationally, it will immediately impose further punishments. The mistress sits in each case at the longer lever and can tinker the truth as she wishes.

"Or do you want to claim that I am lying, slave?" is the question that makes it clear to every sub that he simply cannot win. It is best for the slave in this case to admit his inability and to await his punishment.

124. The secret lettering.

The lady inscribes the slave in such a way that it is impossible for him to read the text. Like the back, for example. You don't have eyes there. The Lady now visits a Femdom party with the slave. The slave will ask himself the whole time what the mistress has written. In addition, the mistress can always arouse the curiosity with hints: Well, if the other ladies find out about you, then... well, well, I don't want to be in your skin....

Or: It's soooooo embarrassing that I wrote this on your back!

Or just before the party: I don't think I should have written that on your back. I think I've gone too far.

The lady does not change anything however on the inscription. It'll drive the slave crazy. A real MindFuck.

Of course, their behaviour turns out to be exaggerated afterwards.

Maybe it's just that the back says something harmless like "I am the slave of Lady X."

If the mistress does not want to attend a party, she can also play the game together with a friend who invites her home.

125. Ruined orgasm by the slave himself.

A ruined orgasm is an orgasm that the slave cannot enjoy because the mistress immediately takes her hands off the penis as soon as he starts ejaculate. No hand, no rubbing, no pleasure. In the first book of ideas we have already dealt with this topic.

Here is the escalation: The slave has to ruin his orgasm himself. You have to let it melt in your mouth!

This task requires the highest degree of discipline and obedience. Probably beginners will be overwhelmed. For there is nothing more mean for a slave than to have to make sure that at the moment of ecstasy, at the moment of the highest happiness, that this lust is transformed into a feeling of dissatisfaction. But it is not only dissatisfaction that the slave feels, in some cases even pain is reported. The slave will twist and wriggle and spasmodically try to follow the mistress' orders and keep his hands under control.

The implementation: The slave jerks off in front of the mistress. If he's close, he asks the mistress submissively for permission. Now the mistress can tease him a bit, refuse to let him orgasm, play a little bit with his hope and make him wriggle. If he is again shortly before and asks for permission, the mistress can give him the orgasm. "Splash, slave," says the mistress and adds the fatal command: "Away with your hands! Now! Get them behind your back!"

The mistress should say this order extremely strictly and consistently. I also recommend that you announce and discuss the scenario beforehand. If the lady surprises the slave with it, even experienced slaves are overtaxed fast. Too strong is their nature to savour the orgasm.

So: Prepare the slave before the session for the ruined orgasm and tune in. According to the motto: "Be glad that you are allowed to relieve yourself. And prove to me that you are capable of being obedient at the decisive moment and not just wanting to satisfy your urge.

The whole thing is an extreme challenge to the obedience of every slave. If it works: Congratulations to the lady, as not every Femdom has such a well-trained slave.

126. Faked Ballbusting.

The lady kicks the slave's balls without warning. Ouch! That hurts right, really hurt. Careful, ladies, we don't want to hurt the slave seriously. This game requires experience, the necessary hardness and empathy. It's not that easy.

Once the first step has been taken, the fun begins. The slave will now - understandably enough - be very afraid of the next step. If he gets the order to spread his legs to offer his soft tissues to the mistress for the next kick, he will have to face the biggest challenge. He'll be scared to death. Even the most experienced Maso-slaves have respect for a ballbusting because it is very painful. No man in the world can remain unimpressed when a woman steps into his balls.

It is particularly attractive to have the slaves tied up defenceless in front of them. For example, he can be attached to a pulley with his arms up, while the mistress stands in front of him and repeatedly deceives him with one leg trying to kick him in his crown jewels. A hard psycho game which is however extremely entertaining for the lady, because she can feel the fear of the slave very clearly.

127. The mobile phone check.

Smartphones are now used more as computers than phones. This results in important, sensitive and often intimate data being stored on the devices. In other words, cell phones are secrets. For most slaves, it is correspondingly unpleasant for them to have to give their mobile phone out of the hand - of course with all passwords and barring codes. The lady must finally be able to check whether the slave also maintains contacts with other ladies. He won't be unfaithful to her, will he?

Even the attempt to claim the mobile phone from the slave is amusing. In the end, it is not about sniffing around in the slave's data, but only about getting him to actually deliver the mobile phone. This is a great sign of trust and should be rewarded accordingly.

I recommend that you only announce your announcement, take a close look at the mobile phone, ask for the mobile phone - and then return it immediately without having had a look at it.

128. The Rice Challenge.

The lady scatters white and brown rice on a plate, mixes the rice grains and asks the slave to separate the rice carefully and to collect it in two bowls.

To make it even more difficult, he may only touch the rice with a pair of tweezers, but not with his dirty slave paws. (Slaves' paws are always dirty, even if they are clean.)

The whole thing requires the slaves highest concentration. It is in the essence of most slaves that they try to do a good job. It is extremely frustrating when they do not receive any praise for it, but rather when they are set up to fail. The lady sabotages his efforts, by giving quite frankly wrong grains in the bowl and then accusing the slaves of working uncleanly. Especially when the slave has already struggled for 20 minutes, this experience is highly unjust and frustrating.

129. The alleged sex and leak slave.

The lady opens to the slave that she will make him available to an attractive girlfriend as sex and tongue slave. Of course, the slave will be happy about it and surely very excited. You can increase the anticipation even more by saying that the slave may serve two or three girlfriends in this way. It is important that the slave really wants to have the mentioned women. The more attractive they are, the better.

The slave is instructed to prepare everything. He has to provide condoms and lubricating gel, to prepare the love nest beautifully and to provide for a pleasant atmosphere (romantic music, sparkling wine, muted light).

Now it's getting serious. As soon as the lady or the ladies arrive, the lady introduces the slave as sex and tongue slave. Solemnly she reveals his privates - suddenly it is very quiet in the room. A lady begins to giggle. "He's tiny!" says another one, unpleasantly touched and seemingly surprised. The ladies are discussing the mini penis and come to the conclusion that this must be a mistake. Such a tiny penis can't satisfy a woman. The slave must be locked into a CB and henceforth serve as a CB slave. A hard blow for the sub-below the belt. Note: it doesn't matter how big the penis of the slave actually is. If the ladies call the penis small, the slave will believe it.

130. Soap for the cheeky mouth.

A slave who was impudent must be punished. But you don't always have to pick a percussion instrument. Even more memorable is a bar of soap. The lady washes his cheeky mouth out.

I'm sure he'll resist. Also the mistress should make sure that he does not take any health risks, swallows and so on. But at least symbolically, it should wash his mouth. An experience the slave will not forget so quickly. Hours after that, he still has the taste of soap in his mouth.

131. Slave problem zones.

Men have the strange quality of being at peace with themselves, even though they should not be. I am referring, for example, to their external appearance.

Raccoon instead of washboard belly? Ah, not so bad, the slave thinks.

The lady sees it differently. In order to show the slave her vision, she places him in front of a mirror and asks him to apologize for everything that comes to his mind.

The lady can strengthen the topic, by marking the problem zones of slaves with a marker. However, I recommend using a water-soluble pencil....

In the end, the slave could realize that he is one big problem area.

132. The chambermaid.

An interesting game for hotel stays. After the overnight stay and the breakfast, the mistress will put her belongings together. In many hotels you have to check out around 12 o' clock, the time suitable for this game is around 10.30 or 11 o' clock.

While the mistress is dressed quite normally in the meantime, the slave must undress. The mistress ties up the sub and introduces him to a dildo. The important thing is that he is unable to free himself under any circumstances. The mistress blindfolds him and makes sure that he really can't see anything anymore. Now he's being gagged. The Mistress announces that she has to go to the reception to inquire about something. The bound slave remains behind.

Suddenly there's a knock. If the lady can adjust her voice well, then she can also call "room service". Since the slave cannot move, he must experience helplessly how the supposed chambermaid finds him. Here the mistress can play with the sounds of her shoes. It should first run purposefully and busily into the room - and then suddenly stop. Maybe you can hear a short expression of her astonishment. A short "Oh!" will do. It stops for a moment. Maybe you will hear the sound of a mobile phone taking pictures shortly afterwards. Then she leaves the room quickly.

Five minutes later the mistress is back. The slave is subjected to an extremely embarrassing scenario in his head. This game is only something for experienced slaves, who are really tolerant and devoted to the mistress under all circumstances.

It is also important that the mistress always has a "Do not Disturb" sign hanging on the room door. Not that the real chambermaid's gonna burst in.

133. Blind flight demonstration.

The slave is presented by the lady to one or more friends. In practice, many women are curious to see such a show, but are stressed and afraid about the unusual situation because they do not know how to behave.

This insecurity can be taken away from many women if one announces that the slave serves with blindfolded eyes. So he can't see the lady or the ladies.

Honestly, I have to say that slaves don't like it at all. He is a visual creature and wants to see women. But if it helps to convince the ladies, you should give it a try.

134. The unknown admirer.

The lady builds up before the slave the picture of an unknown admirer. This is how she stirs up his jealousy and challenges him to peak performance. The whole thing could start, for example, with a splendid bouquet of flowers, which the slave will see one day in the mistress's living room. The slave doesn't have to know that the mistress has sent them himself, including a charming greeting card.

In the following days the mistress proudly presents gifts, which allegedly also come from her admirer. The slave will become more and more jealous - especially when he learns that his mistress gets involved with the admirer.

135. The broken Cane.

A strong symbol of a strict and sadistic femdom is a broken cane. Especially at the beginning of an SM relationship, a seemingly carelessly lying broken cane can be a memorable discovery for the slave. He will be immediately respectful - not to say fearful - of the mistress and will double his efforts to please the lady. After all, he saw with his own eyes what else could happen. In the head of the slave the lady is now a strict sadist, with whom one doesn't joke. The slave has never been so obedient.

Category Humiliation

Many subs love to be humiliated by their mistress. In this category it is about ideas, how the lady can drive the shame blush into the slave's face. It is important to understand the psyche of the slave. Who loves humiliation, for him are slaps in the face of sweet lustful pain. It hurts to get a hard slap, but it excites the slave also.

136. Small Penis Humiliation: the Ice Bag Idea.

It doesn't matter whether his penis is really small or not. Even men with a large penis can be humiliated and laughed at as little tails in this way. Laughing at men because of their (supposedly) small penises hits them in the core of their masculinity. That really hurts!

With the Ice Bag idea, the mistress takes advantage of the fact that the tail becomes smaller in the cold. It is obvious to produce this cold with ice bags. The lady places the slave in bondage and puts ice bags on his penis. On the one hand, this has the effect that the slave will twist in his shackles to escape the cold. In order to prevent his best piece from being damaged, the cold may only affect him for a short time. We don't want him to freeze to death. His penis will react quickly, shrink and hide in the foreskin. Now the mistress can put the ice bags aside and make fun of the tiny penis. How humiliating!

137. Small Penis Humiliation: Tail Comparison.

It is extremely entertaining when the mistress compares her strap-on with the penis of the slave. Preferably the lady should select a strap-on, which clearly surpasses the slave's penis in every respect. Thus the slave is made aware of his inferiority. It is therefore only natural that he submits himself to his mistress as a slave and at least serves her as a subordinate, if he is not able to satisfy a woman with his penis.

The mistress can enjoy this game indefinitely. For example, by repeatedly reminding the slave about how great it is to have a neat cock and how inferior and ridiculous such a tiny slave cock looks.

138. Small Penis Humiliation: Wanking with tweezers.

The slave, the mistress explains, has such a small micro penis that he has to use tweezers if he wants to jerk off.

Exactly this happens: The slave gets a tweezers (with rounded edges) and should jerk off in front of the mistress with it. He may carefully pull the foreskin backwards and play around.

Many slaves will look at the lady inquiringly. They don't know how to use the tweezers for their orgasm. In this case the mistress laughs aloud, takes away the tweezers from him and thinks the slave is too stupid even to jerk off. An extremely embarrassing story, which you have to tell your friends at the next Femdom meeting.

139. Small Penis Humiliation: the magnifying glass.

The lady takes a magnifying glass to the hand and goes on the search for the slave's penis. Where the hell is he? Where can he be? At the end the mistress terminates the search without result. The mini-penis is simply not visible. Maybe she'll come back sometime - with a microscope.

140. Jerking between the toilet seat.

The slave may jerk off - but differently than he has hoped. He may clamp his penis between the toilet seat and stimulate in this way. How embarrassing! If a friend of the mistress would see this... unimaginable....

141. Foreign semen?

The slave may satisfy himself and squirt on a plate. Then he has to lick the sperm, hold it on his tongue and present the sperm covered tongue to the mistress. The mistress takes a photo of it and announces that she will show it to her friends. But with a different story. She will tell that the slave has a secret bi inclination and had satisfied another slave orally.

How embarrassing! Whether the Mistress actually tells her girlfriends this story doesn't matter. The slave believes it and will be accordingly ashamed, that's the point.

142. The Pig Nose Hook.

The slave is made pig with a Pig Nose Hook. In each nostril a hook is attached, which pulls the nose up or back with a thin string. In this way the slave gets a kind of pig's snout. If you want to see a photo, you just have to google for "Pig Nose Hook". You can humiliate the slave wonderfully with it.

Tightening up the slave he can be asked to grunt and squeal like a pig. It becomes extreme when the slave has to marvel at himself in the mirror. Here you have to be psychologically careful that you don't push it too far and don't stamp on the self image of the slave too brutally. In any case, I recommend catching the slave after the session and bring him back to eye level.

Pig Nose Hook "can be bought in SM boutiques. Often there are hooks to this equipment in addition, with which one can keep the mouth of slaves open or distort.

143. The sex doll.

It is really very humiliating if the slave is not allowed to fuck a real woman, but only an inflatable sex doll. Sex dolls are available in almost all sex shops. The coarser and simpler the doll is designed, the more humiliating it is for the sub. The doll gets a name and becomes a real personality, a friend of the slave.

This idea is the ideal way to savour the action with pointed remarks. An increase is the integration in a demonstration. The slave is first shown and at the end of the session he climbs his "girlfriend", the sex doll. Really extremely embarrassing! He's not good enough for a real woman.

144. The artificial vagina.

One variation of the sex doll is the artificial vagina. There are sex toys that can satisfy men's needs. The slave has to kneel before the mistress and satisfy himself with an artificial pussy. Just like the sex doll, the artificial pussy gets a name, for example Chantelle or Angelique. How romantic! I think the two of them have found each other. What a beautiful couple!

145. The shoe sole.

According to my observation, an unbelievable number of slaves are shoe and foot fetishists. High heels and stilettos in particular excite more slaves than you might think. Many other Femdoms have confirmed this assumption to me.

Accordingly, it is mean to keep a slave's fetish in front of him, but not to let him kiss or lick. No, the slave may not worship the high heel and thus satisfy his fetish lust. He must not blow the pointed long heel and should not lovingly kiss and lick the fine material of the shoe. All he can do is lick off the underside of the shoe.

Even slaves who attach great importance to hygiene are ready to be allowed to at least be close to their fetish in this way.

The lady should savour this action with the appropriate verbal eroticism. The slave is simply not worthy to lick and kiss the upper material. All he gets is the sole. The mistress' shoes were never so much in demand after this little game. Psychologically speaking, we always want the most intimate thing that we cannot have.

146. Spitting.

The generic term "spitting" means games with the saliva of the mistress. In some femdom relationships there is no kiss, in the professional domina area for example. As a "substitute" there is the one-sided transfer of the mistress' spit to the sub. The lady spits into his wide open mouth. In combination with slaps and reprimands, spitting is an extreme humiliation, especially when the mistress forbids the slave from wiping the spit from his face. This form of defilement is comparable to the preference of many dominant men to cum over a woman in the face.

147. Target spitting.

A popular game is to instruct the slave to open his mouth wide and now try to hit his mouth while spitting. Often enough the spitting goes wrong and the slave has to endure that the saliva runs down on his face. Only inexperienced Subs have the impulse to wipe the spit off. This can be prevented simply by fixing the slave's hands behind his back.

The mistress can also spit on things and ask the sub to lick the saliva away. The boots or the high heels of the mistress are ideal for this. In this case, the spit serves as a kind of shoe polish.

148. The Gangbang helper.

This idea would also fit into the category „Chastity belt" (CB). The CB slave is sent in the locked state on a gangbang. All men fuck and let themselves blow their tails - but not the slave. In such an environment it is even more humiliating to be kept chaste by the mistress. If the slave wants to remain anonymous, he can wear a mask. However, one should consider that the humiliation is then only half as strong.

The slave can take care of the men's buffet, fresh condoms and lubricating gel are enough or make himself useful.

149. Cuckold services.

As a reminder: A cuckold is a man who takes pleasure from when his wife is sexually fulfilled with another. The other man is, so to speak, putting his horns on him.

This topic becomes even more intense when the cuckold not only tolerates this relationship, but actively promotes it. For example, by paying for the couple's dinner and their hotel room.

Or by cleaning up the apartment where the couple will be enjoying themselves later.

He can also be ordered to iron the man's shirt, who is at the same time eating his wife in the next room in the marriage bed. Or he can even stand next to the bed with condoms and lubricant.

In short, it's about involving the cuckold in the game in such a way that he supports it. In this way, his humiliation grows even greater.

150. The cuckold as a sperm eater.

The idea of cuckolding is to make the slave feel that other men can have the mistress, but not him. The slave derives his lust from this humiliation. This is not for everyone, but for some slaves already (there are surprisingly many who are excited about it).

Another increase is to bring the slave into contact with the Bull, who is allowed to make the mistress sexually happy.

So it is extremely humiliating if the slave has to drink the used condom after the sexual act. Possibly even in front of his rival.

151. Anilingus/Rimming.

Anilingus is the practice of the slave licking the mistress's anus with his tongue. He's kind of licking her ass. This circumstance is perceived by some as humiliating, by others as a pleasurable privilege.

In order to steer the happening in the direction of humiliation, the lady should help with appropriate verbal eroticism. She can say that the slave is not worthy to lick her pussy and may only touch her ass.

Anilingus can be combined wonderfully with face sitting, whereby it is recommended to fix the slave motionlessly. So he is the fully exposed and open to his mistress's desires and she can even determine his breathing air.

The latter should only be done with an experienced mistress who knows what she is doing and who is absolutely trusted.

On the subject of hygiene, the mistress should of course wash well before the anilingus.

The feeling of a licking tongue at the anus is by the way very pleasant. Even if at first in the practice you start to shy away, you should think about it.

152. The slightly different toilet paper.

A more extreme form of anilingus is to use the slave as a kind of toilet paper after going to the toilet. This game is an extreme humiliation and only for very experienced slaves, who are well trained and understand it as an honor to serve the mistress in this way intimately.

153. Sauna with CB.

The lady takes her slave to the sauna. This is an honour for the slave, but also an extreme humiliation when he has to wear a CB. It is important to make sure that the CB is not locked with a metal lock, but with a numbered disposable plastic lock. The metal heats up and can become burning hot.

This measure should only be carried out with a slave who likes public presentation (Public Humiliation).

154. Self-punishment.

The slave shall punish himself in front of the mistress. So hit yourself, pinch yourself, slap your face or use the dildo yourself.

The mistress sits in a relaxed way and watches as the slave gets ready himself. From time to time she spices up the happening with a condescending commentary or encourages the slaves to give it even harder. How embarrassing!

Category

Chastity Control

In the category of CB Training, the chastity of the sub is the focus of attention. If you control a man's penis, you control the whole man. I therefore recommend that every Femdom should pay full attention to this issue.

155. Chastity.

The slave is locked into a CB, a chastity belt. For example, in a CB 6000, it is important that the mistress has bought the lock and the keys herself, otherwise the slave may cheat. There are usually two keys to a lock. Key one is a spare key and can be hidden in the mistress's apartment, for example - for all cases. The lady can carry the key 2 with her. For example, on a ankle chain, a chain around the neck or a bunch of keys. This gives her full control over the sexuality of the slave.

I recommend keeping a diary of the days on which the slave was closed and when he was allowed to come to the climax. It's also interesting why he wasn't allowed to come. I keep such a CB diary for my slave Toytoy in my Femdom-Blog. It is open to the public, you can find the diary here:

http://domina-lady-sas.blogspot.de/p/mein-sklavenstall.html

156. Porno torture.

The mistress sends the chaste slaves generous photos again and again. She can also send links to SM pornos which are available in the net to the slave via e-mail. The slave has to watch the movies - without being able to play around, what a pity!

157. Torment with lust.

Especially with chaste slaves a charming game with the desire: The lady takes off her panties, slaps the legs on top of each other and puts the panties over her high heel. Now she stretches out her leg and the slave is allowed to sniff the panties. He may get horny, but he may not cum - that would also hardly be possible if he wears a CB.

In the following scenario one can pull the Mistress panties over his nose and fix it in bondage. In this way, he is both excited and busy when one wants to dedicate oneself to other things.

158. Satisfy the mistress.

The slave spoils the mistress orally, who sits relaxed on the sofa. For example, with the tongue or a dildo gag. If the lady does not wish intimate insights, she can cover the slave's eyes. The slave satisfies the mistress and has been so well trained by her so that he remains chaste and unsatisfied.

159. CB key rental.

An increase in chastity by the key owner: She does not keep the key herself for a certain period of time, but hands over the CB key to a friend or acquaintance. For the girlfriend it is usually very appealing to sniff into this feeling, what it is like to keep a slave chaste and have the power over his sexuality. It's even more humiliating for the slave. The lady can also let girlfriends vote on whether the slave may come. There are many variations that bring fun and fresh air into chastity.

160. Twitter vote.

It is exceedingly humiliating for the CB-slave, if his mistress lets others decide whether he may come or not. One option is to start a poll on Twitter. I tried that and found it very entertaining. The result was that the slave was allowed to have a ruined orgasm. Well, at least!

161. CB + Viagra.

A chastity cuff is especially interesting in combination with a Viagra tablet. The Viagra tablet would enhance the standing ability of the slave's gland, but the CB prevents that the penis can be proudly erect.

I tried it all with my slave Toytoy. He had the usual symptoms that can be observed in Viagra: slightly reddened eyes, slightly reddened head, very slight headaches and the nose closes slightly because the mucous membranes swell up. Viagra only works if the man is sexually stimulated. The lady can sexually excite the slave for example with her stocking clad feet over the breast and the CB and let the slave suck her toes. The

Toytoy penis continued to swell, stimulated in such a way, but was unable to straighten up because of the CB.

I really enjoyed this dilemma, which I brought the slave into. I think you have to be careful with this game so that the slave doesn't endure any damage. It is the responsibility of the mistress to catch up with the slave immediately if he can no longer endure it or if there are complications. Implementation at your own risk as always, this remains an experiment - but also a very interesting one.

162. Massage without happy end.

The lady sends the CB-slave to a massage parlor. Here he can enjoy the erotic arts of a lady - but it will be extremely embarrassing for him to have to out himself in front of the lady as a CB slave. Can you do that? I think so, because discretion is the top priority in a massage parlor. It will be a sweet humiliation for the CB slave to have to reveal himself as a sub to the young, pretty lady. Furthermore, such a massage is a permanent tease & denial for him.

163. Eroticism without happy ending.

The massage without a happy end can be further enhanced by sending the mistress to a brothel where he has to pay a lady for her services. However, he will have little pleasure in their service with the CB. It is also extremely embarrassing to date a woman for a nap and then not be able to get to the point. The slave is extremely humiliated by this.

164. Ruined orgasm.

A great fun - especially if the slave doesn't know about the ruined orgasm yet.

The slave is kept chaste in a CB for some time. Then he is unlocked and allowed to lie on his back at the feet of the mistress who is enthroned in front of him. The slave's hands are tied together at the cuffs and are connected with the leash. The mistress holds the leash in her hand while the slave jerks to her feet. If the slave is close to it, he must ask the lady for permission. The mistress finally allows him to come, but pulls the leash up at this moment, so that the slave cannot satisfy himself any longer. The beautiful feeling is lost by jerking off, the sperm shoots out of the tail without any satisfaction. His orgasm is ruined.

This topic is new to you? Then I'll be happy to explain it in more detail. Satisfaction with orgasm arises from the fact that the slave can jerk off his penis when he comes. Jerking with the hand is nothing more than a replacement for the movement in the vagina during sexual intercourse.

With the ruined orgasm it is now so that in the moment the slave starts to squirt, the jerking is stopped. His penis is no longer touched. The slave cannot suddenly stop the orgasm. It is now - even without jerking - sperm is thrown out of the penis. This physical reaction is no longer controllable and takes place automatically. But: the beautiful feeling is lost. It can even be painful if the slave no longer jerks off or is jerked off while ejaculating. He hangs in the air, so to speak, and has to endure the orgasm. Afterwards, he feels liberated, the pressure is gone, but he does not feel satisfied. It's called a ruined orgasm.

165. Maid.

The CB slave is feminised and dressed up as a maid. He wears a maid outfit for that. It is important to reinterpret every part of him. His penis is now called "clitoris" or "clit" for short, his anus is called "ass cunt" and his nipples are called "titties". The slave gets a woman's name and has to learn to move like a woman and to go elegantly on high heels. Common make-up in front of the mirror is one of the most amusing things about feminisation.

Especially humiliating is the mistress who shows him off at a party. The masculinity of the slave has disappeared, he is more woman than man. The game can be continued by practicing with the maid how to satisfy cock. The upbringing of maids is the next step after chastity. Here the slave's masculinity is completely denied.

166. Feminized into the office.

The slave has to wear a female garment under his male clothes. For example, pink panties or stockings without suspenders. In this way he is humiliated, but not publicly exposed.

As a first test, he can only wear the clothes for a short time while shopping.

The mistress can send messages to him on the mobile phone, in which she addresses him with his female name and makes fun of him, in order to increase the humiliation even further.

167. Freeze the key.

This game is especially entertaining when you watch the reaction of the sub. In front of his eyes, his CB key is placed in an ice cube mould and placed in the refrigerator's freezer compartment. The slave sees: A quick redemption is no longer possible. Finally, it will take some time for the ice to thaw out for the key to be available again. This game is another example of a tunnel game.

168. Cuckold game.

A cuckold is a man who takes pleasure from the fact that his wife cheats and humiliates him with another man. It is also said that he has his horns raised. It doesn't have to come to the sex right away. The mistress can also meet her admirer in a bar and have a drink with him in front of the cuckold. Then the cuckold has to settle the score. The clearer it becomes for other guests that the lover humiliates the actual partner by seducing his wife in front of his eyes, the more embarrassing the whole thing is.

You can increase this game by actually having sex between mistress and lover. Before the love play the lady humiliates the CB-slave, by pointing out the advantages of her lover and shows the slave these, explicitly pointing out how inferior he is compared to her lover. A classic example is the tail comparison between lover and cuckold. The cucki has to serve the couple drinks and provide condoms. The cuckold has to pay for the hotel room where the meeting takes place. The further he gets to be on the date, the more humiliating it is for him. His mistress lives out her sexuality with another man while he remains celibate and chaste.

Note: We women love harmony. For this reason, many women tend to meet the two men at eye level. I advise against it. It is easier if it is clear from the outset who has which role to play. For example, you can give the slave a seat in the bar and order him/her to order a peppermint tea while sipping cocktails with your lover. I don't think it makes sense to have a conversation between the men.

169. Eat ice cream.

This game is amusing and at the same time a benefit for the soul. The lady buys a delicious ice cream and eats it in front of the CB-slaves. He will only be able to think of one thing when he leaks the ice and will suffer accordingly. And double so much because the ice cream is only for the mistress. The mistress should occasionally become aware of why she eats the ice cream and accordingly use her tongue. I know you can forget everything around you while eating ice cream...

170. Prostate drainage.

The prostate drainage is used to take pressure away from the CB-slave without giving him the satisfaction of a full-fledged orgasm. The mistress makes sure that the slave has cleaned himself with an enema. She inserts her index or middle finger carefully into the anus of the slave. Use plenty of lubricating gel and sterile disposable gloves. Nice and slow. The anus is very sensitive and there is a risk of injury if you use force.

The finger of the lady now palpates the prostate of the slave. It is about two or three centimeters in the rectum. The prostate can be recognized as a small depression, it feels spongy. Now the mistress strokes along the prostate with slight pressure again and again. This is the prostate drainage. It shouldn't take more than a minute.

If the drainage is too painful or too unpleasant for the slave he should say this clearly and the mistress should in this case immediately carefully and sensitively stop.

In my opinion, drainage can only be done with one finger, a dildo is not suitable for this because it is a matter of feeling.

The slave has to ask permission before squirting or leaking. While he comes, the mistress takes her hands from the penis and does not allow the slave to touch himself. His orgasm will be ruined. To make sure that the slave doesn't touch himself with his hands the mistress can fix him motionlessly.

171. The Moods of a Diva.

Another variation to the Tease- and Denial is to catch up with the slave after a particularly good performance and to let him jerk off as a reward. The slave must have the impression that he is to be rewarded for his good performance.

The mistress commands him to ask her for permission before he cums. Full of hope, the sub will ask the mistress for it. Now the lady instructs him completely surprisingly to put his hands behind the back immediately. She says she has changed her mind. She doesn't have to give a reason. It's just a mood. Men hate these sudden moods and mood swings. The slave is locked again. Whether he begs or not. The mistress must not allow herself to be softened under any circumstances. Thus the slave is made perfectly clear that he is completely dependent on the hand of the Mistress and on her moods. She can do whatever she wants with him.

172. The Cube.

Chastity belt slaves (CB-slaves) crave for nothing so much as to be allowed to wank. The mistress is doing them a favor. The slave gets a cube (or two) and rolls the dice. The number of dots is the number of wank movements he can perform on his cock with his hand. If he rolls a four with a root, he is allowed to jerk his penis four times up and down. In any case, this is clearly not enough to reach the climax. The slave gets a minimal taste of how beautiful masturbation feels. But this is also accompanied by a severe punishment, because after the short erection his penis is locked again. Maybe he'll be allowed to roll the dice again tomorrow - if he's a good boy.

173. The dildo-teasing.

The CB slave kneels in front of the sofa and has to see how the lady spoils herself with a dildo. She can also tease him by comparing the dildo to the slave's mini-penis. Since the slave doesn't deserve it, she has to enjoy herself in a different way. For the slave this is an action between heaven and hell. He enjoys seeing his mistress like this - but is condemned to passive watching and cannot give himself any satisfaction.

174. The lingerie tease.

The lady pulls a worn panty in such a way over the nose of the CB-slave that he has the smell of the lady directly in front of his nose. Later she can put the lingerie in his mouth as a gag. Stimulating, but also degrading.

175. The bath of the mistress.

The slave is instructed to prepare the mistress a beautiful bath in the bathtub. He has to make a real effort and decorate the bathroom sensually. For example, with candles, rose petals and a fine bubble bath to pleasantly temper water.

The lady enjoys the bath naked. A circumstance that shouldn't leave the CB slave cold. It becomes even more difficult for him if the mistress moves seductively, kneads her breasts or if he may even kiss one of her feet.

176. The destroyed CB keys.

The locks for chastity belts are usually supplied with two keys. The mistress should keep one key in her apartment for security reasons, the other one she can always carry with her. For example, on a key ring or a cute anklet.

The mistress now secretly has a third and fourth key made. Once she is really angry with the slave she can do the following. She scolds the slave and announces to keep him chaste forever. Her patience is at an end, the slave will never again cum and stay in the CB forever.

The slave will not believe that his mistress is so cruel. So she shows him the evidence and gives him the two keys. He may insert the keys into the lock and unlock it. He then realizes that these are actually his keys. The CB is closed and the two keys are destroyed in front of the horrified slave. The slave will be panicked with fear. Was that it? Will he really have to stay in the CB forever?

In the end, the Mistress saves him and shows him the two new keys.

Category PartyPlay

This category is about ideas on how to play with a slave at a BDSM party. It is particularly attractive to include other femdoms in the game. Be sure to invite only those ladies you trust and who are reliable and responsible to play. After all, you are responsible for your slave and must make sure that his health is not endangered at any time. If you take this point seriously and always pay attention to choosing the right players, then these party games are great fun and provide a lot of good humour and topics for conversation.

177. Animals.

An entertaining party game is to let the slaves imitate animals. He should not only use his voice to imitate the sounds of animals, but also his facial expressions and his whole body.

Here are some specific suggestions.

"Grunt like a pig, slave! Show the mistresses your little striped tail!"

"You're a puppy. Show us how nice you bark, doggy! Go on, fetch the crop, doggie!"

"You're a cow. Come on, what's a cow do? Louder! You have to moo louder! We all want to hear it!"

"As stupid as you are, you must be a sheep. A black sheep, yes, you are. Well? How does a sheep sound? Louder! We all want to hear you."

"You want to be a stallion? No way! You're a mare. Come on, like a mare. Make it loud so that the stallions can hear you..."

178. Shoe-shine-boy.

The slave gets the task to clean the boots of the mistress with his penis as cleaning cloths. He has to take his penis like a cloth in both hands and rub it over the shoe and polish it until shiny. This works best with leather shoes.

Very humiliating when another party member is watching. Perhaps you would like to offer another Femdom to have her boots or shoes polished as well?

This game can be pushed further by instructing the slave to use his own and very special „shoe polisher" for shoe care.

179. Labelling.

Mark the slave with a water-based pencil. For example, write "useless" on his penis or draw arrows on his butt, pointing to his hole and write "fuckhole" over it.

A beautiful, inspiring party game. Every mistress is allowed to arm herself with a pencil and let off steam at the slave. Experience shows that you should play the game towards the end of the party, because the slave looks rather stupid after that due to the many labels. After the inscription you can free the slave from the inscriptions under the shower.

More ideas for lettering:

Property of Lady X "on the bottom or over the penis.

„Slave" on the chest.

„Wanker" on the hand with which the slave masturbates.

„Face slap face" on one cheek.

180. Catch rings.

The lady inserts a double dildo or something like that in the ass. It is important that the object sticks out far. The slave must stretch his butt out and hold it up high. The party guests now throw rings over the end.

Extremely entertaining for the ladies and humiliating for the slave. Every ring that finds its target gives a point. The lady who scores 5 points first wins.

The rings are available as toys, for example. Search the internet under the keyword "Ring Throwing Game" to find the matching rings.

An alternative to the object in the bottom is the other side: the stiff penis of the slave. That works wonderfully, too. However, the penis must remain stiff for some time. If the slave should not be able to do this, it becomes embarrassing quickly....

181. Synchronize porn.

It is very entertaining to watch porn at the party, turn off the sound and instruct the slave to synchronize all actors and actresses. It's wonderfully stupid when a slave synchronizes female porn stars and mimics her moaning.

182. Big jerks.

At least two subs are required for this game. The slaves kneel next to each other and are allowed to jerk off under the eyes of the Femdoms. Whoever squirts the furthest wins. All losers have to clean up their juice and are chastised by the Femdoms with the crop or other instruments. The winner gets a reward.

183. Ruined orgasm.

We've already looked at what a ruined orgasm is. With this variant the slave is fixed naked on a stretching rack or a stable kitchen table or desk. Now his penis is coated with lubricating gel and wiped by the ladies present . Very soft, slow and tender, sometimes only at the top, sometimes hard, fast and demanding - varied.

The art is to stimulate the slave with a few quick, intense hand movements over the point where he can no longer control himself. At this moment all women take away their hands and the slave shoot his sperm on his chest or belly. He will make fuck movements in the air, but since there is nothing to fuck except air, he will not be able to draw satisfaction from salvation. His orgasm is ruined.

184. Slave tennis.

This SM game is based on tennis. Two femdoms are the players, the slave is the ball. The sub kneels on the floor. A mistress slaps him in the face and the slave has to move like a beaten tennis ball - in front of the other mistress' feet. She also beats him and the slave moves back to the first mistress. The whole thing lives from the slave's ability to represent a good tennis ball and is often extremely entertaining.

185. Demonstration.

A very nice party game, which you can also play in threesome, with two ladies and one slave. The second lady doesn't necessarily have to be dominant, it is enough if she watches with interest.

One possible scenario is, for example, that the lady invites the second lady to coffee and cake. One meets first without the slave and exchanges. Then the lady leads the slave in naked on a leash. To increase his humiliation even further, he can, for example, wear his CB. The slave has to greet the second lady by kissing her shoes.

The lady introduces the slave, describes, since when she has him, explains his strengths and weaknesses (especially the weaknesses!) and humiliates him in front of the other lady, by talking intimately about his last orgasms.

The slave has to accept all this and has to prove by exercises how well he is trained. These can be simple things such as walking on the leash at foot or jerking off on command.

The lady can involve the second lady and even allow her to use the slave. This is best discussed in advance. It is important to make it very clear to the second lady which taboos the slave has. I recommend giving her this in writing, otherwise she can easily pretend at the end that she had simply misunderstood or that the mistress had not expressed herself clearly.

If one does not have any confidence in the second mistress yet, one should not leave the slave unsupervised. As always, the mistress is responsible for the slave and has to make sure that nothing happens to him.

Especially at parties, a demonstration is a highlight, which always provides a lot of fun.

186. Auction.

The slave is first shown to the party and then auctioned off - for an amount of less than $10, because he is not worth more. This should be clear to him and brought to his attention.

Now the slave is handed over to the mistress. The slave will be afraid that his taboos might get hurt. This fear should not be taken away from him. Rather, the mistress should strengthen his fears and let him know that the mistress who bought him at auction is a particularly strict lady, who makes the highest demands.

The Femdoms secretly discussed in advance exactly who buys the slave and what taboos and preferences he has.

So everything is well prepared and planned. In front of the slave, however, a scenario is built up as if everything had come spontaneously and as if his new owner is a really strict Femdom.

187. Recognize the handwriting.

With blindfolded eyes the slave kneels in the slave position on the ground. Upright, legs apart, hands with palms open upwards on thighs. The head is upright. The mistresses walk around him, so that he no longer knows which mistress is standing where in the room. Now one of the mistresses slaps the slave and the slave must guess whose handwriting it was.

The slave can start with 10 penalty points. Any correct answer will result in a penalty point being cleared. Every wrong answer adds a penalty point accordingly. As soon as the slave has gotten rid of all penalty points he gets a reward.

188. Detect feet.

Ideal for foot fetishists and those who want to become it. The slave may first of all follow his passion and kiss, massage and sniff the feet of two or more mistresses. He must get really familiar with the feet of the mistresses.

Then his eyes are blindfolded. One mistress takes place on the sofa or chair in front of him and the slave must guess which feet he is kissing. If he's wrong, he'll get penalty points.

There are many variations to this game. Thus one can also train the slave purely on the smell of the mistresses or forbid him to use his hands. You can also put your feet in his mouth and let him recognize the taste of your feet later. Experience has shown that the best results are achieved if the slave is allowed to use all his senses.

189. Fetch-Competition.

Two or more slaves kneel before the mistress. The mistress throws a ball or a dildo away and calls out: "Fetch!". All slaves must now crawl towards the object as quickly as possible and try to retrieve it with their mouths. They are not allowed to use their hands. Whoever returns the object to the mistress in his mouth gets a point. The first player to collect 5 points wins and is rewarded. All others will be punished.

190. Provoke jealousy.

Competition stimulates business. And your relationship, too. Sometimes SM relationships threaten to fall asleep because both partners are too sure not to be replaced. Correspondingly, they don't make any more efforts and the relationship becomes boring.

One way of countering this is to make your partner jealous. A party's a good place for that. Deal with another sub and make sure that your slave is aware of this. It can be a harmless game. For example, let the feet be massaged and show clearly how much you like it and how well the other slave serves you. Watch your sub's reactions secretly.

191. GangSpit.

What the Bukkake is to MaleDoms, that's the GangSpit to Femdoms. At the GangSpit the mistresses spit into the slave's face or also into the opened mouth, if they wish it.

The game is a strong humiliation and one should discuss clearly with the slave in advance if he is willing to undergo this.

192. GangBang.

The GangBang is also available for Femdoms. The slave is fixed on a bench (if there is no one, a massive table will do it, over which the slave has to bend). He is instructed to stretch his butt out far and is then taken by the ladies one after the other with the strapons. At the same time you can also use the slave orally.

If you want to build up the GangBang in the same way as with women, then you let the slave kneel in the circle of the mistresses at the beginning and let him first of all suck the strapons. He has to make the cocks hard and get the mistresses in the mood.

The next step is the actual anal penetration.

For preparation, an enema and a buttplug are recommended, so that the slave is pre-stretched. Also, a lot of lubricant should be used for the GangBang. Be careful not to overdo the banging: the anus is sensitive and there is risk of injury.

193. Punishment Alley.

Some ladies arm themselves with canes and form an alley: the punishment alley. The slave must crawl slowly through this alleyway and is beaten by the mistresses.

You can increase the difficulty level by having the slave crawl through the alley with a glass of water in his hand. His task is to get to the end of the alley with a full glass of water, despite the blows.

When the ladies are really angry, they let him fight his way to the finish line - then a lady kicks the glass with a quick, courageous movement out of the slave's hand. Mistresses can sometimes be quite nasty....

194. The Impossible Shoe Kiss with a second Lady.

A lot of slaves have a weakness for high heels and love it when they are allowed to kiss and lick the object of their desires.

With the impossible shoe kiss the mistresses use this preference, in order to bring the slave into a dilemma, from which there is no escape. A lady commands the slave to crawl to her and worship her shoe. Now a second lady turns up and asks the slave to crawl to her and kiss her shoes. The slave is trapped. Whatever he does, he can only lose. If he follows the order of the second lady, he violates the first lady's demand. She didn't tell him to stop after all. When he crawls to the second lady, she has to protest loudly and surprisingly. However, she is not allowed to complain to the second lady, but to the slave.

If the slave ignores the wish of the second lady, however, this is only wrong and must be punished accordingly.

The more ladies take part and the more demands are made and orders are given from all sides on the slave, the more confused, desperate and guilt-conscious he will feel.

195. Ketchup fun.

Many men are keen to shoot their sperm into women's faces. A gesture of dominance that raises him above the woman. There are several ways to turn this Bukkake game around. We already got to know the version with the spitting. At least as dirty is it to circle the slave and hold a plastic ketchup package as if a woman had a penis. The slave must present his face. The mistress moans as if she were coming like a man. The lady shoots the ketchup from the container into the face of the slave. He has to swallow it all and lick up the remains of the ketchup.

It's a nice mess, but it's incredibly fun. The slave is responsible for the cleaning of course.

196. Public interrogation.

The slave has to answer to the party members. The aim of the FemDoms is to embarrass the slave with their questions.

Which hand do you jerk off with, slave?

What do you think about when you do it to yourself?

Have you ever drunk your Mistress' pee?

You can ask anything.

The slave must not refuse, but must answer honestly and openly. If he refuses, a severe punishment threatens.

The interrogation can be flavored with punishment units to loosen the slave's tongue.

197. Public Tribunal.

A public tribunal is a kind of trial. Such gatherings were held, for example, in the OWK, the Other World Kingdom. The slave was accused of an offence by his mistress. He was brought before the high court and had to admit his guilt publicly. Denial didn't help, because he was condemned in any case. Who believes a slave?

Now you don't need to have a judge's robe to hold such a tribunal - just a little bit of imagination and fun with the game.

The slave is the accused, the mistress the plaintiff. Another lady takes over as the strict prosecutor, who interrogates the slave and questions him. Another mistress is appointed judge. This distribution of roles should be clarified in advance, otherwise the scenario will be shaken.

The tribunal may allow the slave to speak before the sentence. For example, to confess everything, to ask for mercy or to make a statement that should alleviate the situation. It remains to be seen whether the court will be impressed by this.

198. All except you.

At the party the mistress takes care of other slaves generously and allows each one to cum. Every slave may cum - only your own slave may not. How frustrating and mean!

199. Slave theatre.

This game is extremely entertaining and perfect for parties. The slave is to perform a session in front of the assembled ladies with a person who is spontaneously determined by the audience. For example, the audience can choose Angelina Jolie. Or a politician, singer, sportswoman, presenter or something like that.

The slave must now adjust his voice accordingly and play both roles: that of the domina and that of the slave. The whole thing depends on the acting and creative talent of the sub, but it can be very funny even if the slave has no talent at all.

200. Slave competition.

Letting slaves fight each other is an exciting affair. The basic question is: Which slave is the best?

How to answer this question depends on what one understands by „the best". If you want a sub that is very resilient, you can subject the slaves to punishment and see who is most resilient.

Who can take the most blows?

Who is willing to suffer most for his mistress?

Who can take the heaviest weight on the testicles?

The Femdoms find out at the slave competition.

Fine, that's it. You just read 200 ideas. I hope you enjoyed reading it and found some interesting suggestions for you.

Contact and Feedback

Do you have any exciting ideas that are not here?
Please send me an e-mail at madamesaskia@web.de.
I am curious.

I'd also be very interested to know how you like the book.
Write to me personally at my e-mail address
madamesaskia@web.de or leave a review on amazon.

I also invite you to visit my Femdom blog, where I have
put together many interesting interviews with
professional and private dominas for you and also
present my own point of view:

http://domina-lady-sas.blogspot.de/

More from Lady Sas

I have recorded my experiences and the education of my personal slave Toytoy in some books. They have been published on amazon as paperback and eBook. Search amazon for the keyword "Lady Sas" to get my books displayed. For example:

"Suddenly Domina - my secret life as a private domina"

This book tells how it all began. Lady Sas is a private BDSM Mistress from Frankfurt in Germany. In her book she allows the reader to share her private BDSM play, and provides a graphic and vivid description of how she trains and uses her slave. (Not for faint-hearted readers!) The narrative and literal climax of the book is her joint session with Lady Cornelitas, in which her slave is taken to his physical and psychological limit – and even beyond…

„Exchange of Slaves"

Domina Lady Sas is a private Mistress from Frankfurt in Germany. After her first book "Suddenly Dominatrix", where she describes her first steps, she now reports as an experienced and strict Mistress about a very special game. She exchanges slaves with the attractive, sadistic Lady Judith in a hotel in Hamburg. Lady Sas is now in control of the beautiful slavegirl Lisa. And Lady Judith can dominate und use slave Toytoy. In her report Lady Sas shares the night in a very open and frank way.

Bonus

"Suddenly Domina - my secret life as a private domina"

Chapter 1: Back to the beginning.

"SEVENTEEN!!!!!!"

"EIGHTEEN!!!!!"

"NINETEEN!!!!!"

"TWENTY!!!!!!"

"TWENTY-ONE!!!!"

"That's enough for now," I remark casually, and spare him the next stroke. Toytoy's ass clearly bears the mark of my whip, glowing bright and red, as we admire our handiwork.

Together, we untie him. He instinctively falls to the floor and showers Cornelitas' vinyl boots and my leather high heels with alternate kisses to express his gratitude.

"You'd better do it properly, or we'll tie you up again..." I snap. "And don't forget my heel, slave."

"The harsher you treat them, the more submissive they become," Cornelitas observes with a smile.

"It's interesting that you mention that," I reply. "I've noticed the same thing."

"I'm disappointed with you, slave," Cornelitas says firmly, as she looks down on Toytoy, who's still submissively kissing and licking our footwear. "I really expected more from you. You're like a little sissy girl that can't take any pain. You're just a snivelling little whiner: 'Please, Lady Cornelitas...! Mercy, Madame, mercy...! I beg you...! Please Lady Cornelitas...' — "Your constant moaning and begging for mercy was simply embarrassing. Very embarrassing, indeed!"

I look at Cornelitas in surprise. She is twisting the facts to suit herself! It's an interesting technique.

"Aren't you ashamed to be such a wimp? You couldn't even take five strokes without complaining. That's pathetic! What an embarrassment you are."

"Please forgive me, Mistress," Toytoy begs with clenched teeth and a hint of irony in his voice. He clearly feels provoked. He had taken his beating bravely and now Cornelitas is claiming that he hadn't.

"What's that?! Do I hear resentment and rebellion in your voice? Kneel, slave!"

She takes a quick step forward and lets loose a shower of slaps on Toytoy, as he cowers before her. Then she quickly steps back again and offers him her boot.

Toytoy immediately obeys, and shows his submission by obediently kissing and licking her shining footwear.

"You seem a bit rebellious sometimes, slave! Am I right?"

"Yes, Lady Cornelitas. Please forgive me, Lady Cornelitas," Toytoy replies in the same defiant voice.

"Behave!" I hiss angrily. "Remember what I told you!"

"Don't worry," Cornelitas reassures me, "we both understand each other very well. We're just playing —

aren't we, slave? Oh, I still have some dirt on my shoe..."
She points to her heel.

"I need to go to the bathroom," Cornelitas says and winks at me.

"It's over there," I reply and point in that direction.

She laughs. "What I wanted to say was: Has your slave been trained for toilet service?"

"Ehem... not yet," I reply hesitantly. Toilet service? That can't actually be what I think it is, I wonder.

"I understand," says Cornelitas. She takes hold of his leash and pulls Toytoy close to her.

"Would it be beyond your limits if I would piss down on you, slave?" — Yes, she actually uses the word 'piss'.

Toytoy shakes his head.

"Good!" Cornelitas says triumphantly. "Because that is exactly what I intend to do!"

Still holding his leash, she walks assertively to the bathroom, dragging Toytoy behind her. I really want to follow, but somehow don't have the courage to do so.

As if she could read my mind, Cornelitas calls out to me: "You can come and watch, Saskia – if you want to."

I pull myself together and follow them to the bathroom.

My slave is kneeling in the shower.

"Would you mind if I release him from his chastity?" asks Cornelitas. I nod in agreement and give her the key. She unlocks his CB6000, removes all the parts and places them carefully on the bathroom cabinet. Then she lifts her skirt and removes her panties. As I watch, I sense a tingling feeling in my pussy.

Cornelitas stands over the slave and spreads her legs. She places her hands on her hips and asks him: "Have you ever been pissed on, slave?"

To my great surprise, I hear him reply: "Yes, Lady Cornelitas."

"Aha! And who was it who pissed on you?"

"Eh... it happened when I visited some professional femdom studios," Toytoy answers hesitantly.

Without warning, Cornelitas slaps him hard across the face. Or, to judge by the sound it might be more appropriate to say that she whacks him.

"I asked you WHO peed on you, not WHERE," she rebukes him imperiously.

"By Miss Emelie... Lady Silvana de Maart... Lady Pia... Lady Silvia..."

"Aha!" Cornelitas exclaims, "so you're an experienced studio slave. And you like to let ladies piss on you. Do you also drink their piss?"

My slave shakes his head.

"Does Lady Saskia use you as her toilet?"

Again, my slave shakes his head — and my head turns red with embarrassment.

"Would you like her to use you as her toilet?" Cornelitas continues.

Toytoy nods. Wow! My mind races as I take in what I have just learned.

"So you want to feel Lady Saskia's warm nectar on your body? You want to be her dirty little piss-pot?"

Again Toytoy nods in agreement.

"Answer me," Cornelitas says and whacks him across the face a second time.

"Yes, Lady Cornelitas."

"And would you like to take her champagne in your mouth? Would you like to drink her golden nectar like a dirty, greedy little pig?"

"No, Madame."

I am relieved to hear that.

"But if she ordered you to do this for her, would you drink her champagne?"

"Yes, Madame."

"Well spoken," Cornelitas says and gently strokes his cheek. "That is very obedient of you."

"So, would you also drink my piss if I ordered you to do so, slave?"

"No, Madame."

Cornelitas laughs loudly.

"I like you," she says and gently strokes his head. "You have a good sense of humour. But now it's time for a serious answer: Would you also swallow my piss, slave?"

Toytoy shakes his head insistently. "I'm afraid not, Lady Cornelitas."

I feel the tension in the air. How would Cornelitas react to this provocation?

"You do understand that today I am also your Mistress, slave?"

"Yes, Lady Cornelitas, but drinking pee is really one of my taboos", Toytoy explains.

"Aha... but you are still willing to swallow Lady Saskia's pee, so it isn't really a taboo? Or did I miss something?"

"Yes, Lady Cornelitas"

"Are you saying that you don't like me?" Cornelitas' voice is no longer as calm as it was earlier. She sounds offended.

"I like you very much, Madame."

"Aha. And why should I believe you?" She looks at Toytoy inquiringly. "Very well. Enough small talk. Take your pathetic cock and jerk it for me... yes... show me how big it can get... very good... watch out, it's about to come..."

She stands over the slave, who is jerking his cock faster and faster.

I stand by the door and observe the scene. My thoughts start to wander. And I think back to how everything began. Toytoy and I are in an SM relationship. The abbreviation "SM" sounds harmless. Like "WC", "TV" or "ABS". However, when it is spelled out as "sadism and masochism" it has a very different ring. And that is precisely what it means. In this book I would like to tell the story of how I became what I am today: a private dominatrix.

At the end of this book I have added a glossary that explains some important concepts from the world of BDSM. Uninitiated readers can look up the meaning of specialist terms that are used in the text. For example:

BDSM —

Abbreviation for bondage and discipline, dominance and submission, sadism and masochism.

(...)

(End of Excerpt)

Impressum

Domina Lady Sas: 200 Ideas for BDSM Sessions.
Mistress – Slave.

November 2017

Frankfurt/Main, Germany

By Lady Sas

Contact: madamesaskia@web.de

Illustration: Shutterstock

Code: 11 99 43

Printed in Great Britain
by Amazon